It just seemed wrong, somehow, without her

As if there was ... ... it would be mor...

There was a kn... ... open and gave h... ... to get you,' he said, and she smiled back and went up on tiptoe and kissed his cheek.

'I'm sorry. I just had some things I needed to do. How far have you got—oh! It's looking lovely!'

'Not really. It's a bit sparse and a bit lopsided—but, hey. We did it.'

She gave him an encouraging smile. 'You just need a few more little things on it. Oh—what's this?'

'I made it at school,' Rory told her. 'It's an angel.'

It was a pretty scruffy angel, he thought. Kate, though, didn't seem to think any such thing.

She placed it in a prominent position, then rummaged in the box, came up with more red baubles and a fairy, and after they'd put the baubles on she made James stand on a chair and hold Freya up so she could put the fairy on the top.

'There!' she exclaimed, laughing. 'Now it's finished.' And she took Freya from him and swung her round, which gave him time to straighten the fairy before he got down and put the chair away.

And swallow the lump in his throat.

Caroline Anderson has the mind of a butterfly. She's been a nurse, a secretary, a teacher, run her own soft-furnishing business, and now she's settled on writing. She says, 'I was looking for that elusive something. I finally realised it was variety, and now I have it in abundance. Every book brings new horizons and new friends, and in between books I have learned to be a juggler. My teacher husband John and I have two beautiful and talented daughters, Sarah and Hannah, umpteen pets, and several acres of Suffolk that nature tries to reclaim every time we turn our backs!' Caroline also writes for the Mills & Boon® Romance series.

A MUMMY FOR CHRISTMAS

BY
CAROLINE ANDERSON

MILLS & BOON
Pure reading pleasure™

First published in Great Britain 2008
Harlequin Mills & Boon Limited,
Eton House, 18-24 Paradise Road, Richmond, Surrey TW9 1SR

© Caroline Anderson 2008

ISBN: 978 0 263 86362 8

Set in Times Roman 10½ on 12¾ pt
03-1208-51283

Printed and bound in Spain
by Litografia Rosés, S.A., Barcelona

A MUMMY
FOR CHRISTMAS

CHAPTER ONE

'AH. MR MCEWAN. Good of you to join us.'

James stifled a growl of frustration and nailed a smile firmly on his face. 'Sorry I'm late. I was held up in HR—some technical hitch with my registration.'

'So I gather. Sorted now?'

'It is.' And it wouldn't have arisen if he'd remembered to post the damn form back to the hospital once he'd completed it, but hey-ho. And now this dark-haired dynamo with eyes the colour of toffee was gunning for him. His boss.

He swallowed his pride and joined the group gathered round the nursing station. A doctor, two nurses—and the woman. Kate Burgess, consultant general surgeon and his reluctant boss. Well, she wasn't the only one who was reluctant. He managed a more genuine smile for the others. 'Hi—I'm James. Good to meet you all. So—what are we doing?'

The dynamo arched one of those elegant, fine brows and speared him with a look. 'We? Well, *I'm* about to take a patient to Theatre.'

'Then I would imagine I'm assisting you? They said you were expecting me.'

'I was. An hour ago. As it is, I've taken Jo away from her job to do yours.'

He forced a smile. Actually it wasn't hard. What was hard was making sure it didn't look like a smile of relief, because he wouldn't be trapped in Theatre with her in this clearly combative mood. 'Why don't I do Jo's job, then, since I have nothing else that I'm expecting to do and it's fairly pointless for me to join you in Theatre without some kind of introduction to the patient—'

'Which you would have had if you'd been here on time.'

'Well, you need to talk to HR about that,' he said a little tightly, conscious of the interested and speculative looks they were attracting from the rest of the team. Damn her, how dare she give him a public dressing down?

'I did—a form you failed to return,' she said, her voice softer but nevertheless as sharp as a razor. 'Not a good start, McEwan. Paperwork is important.'

He hung on to his temper with difficulty. 'I am aware of that.'

'Good—so I won't need to labour the point. Right, Jo, since Mr McEwan is now here, perhaps you'd like to carry on with what you were supposed to be doing while I fill him in, and then he can assist me in Theatre, as he seems to be so keen.'

'Sure.' Jo smiled at him, pocketed her pen and headed for the door, winking at him as she shouldered it open. He chuckled under his breath. Oh, well, at least he had one ally in the department.

'Right,' she said, and fixed him with those toffee-coloured eyes. The sort of toffee you broke your teeth on. Or maybe your career.

'I'm about to do a hemicolectomy on a patient with a primary tumour in the terminal ileum,' she said, and he felt cold sweat break out all over his body. Oh, God. No. Stick to the plot, he told himself as she went on, 'Stephen Symes, aged fifty-four, been experiencing abdo pain, alternate bouts of diarrhoea and constipation, he's been fast-tracked but was admitted yesterday with vomiting and rectal bleeding.'

He didn't need to hear the list. He knew it by heart.

No! Stop thinking about it. Focus. Focus.

'Scan shows a mass which is almost totally obstructing the terminal ileum and attaching to the peritoneum over the femoral artery—hence the emergency surgery—but we won't really know exactly the extent of it until we open him up, or even if we can do anything at all. It could be tricky, which is why he's our only patient this morning.' She smiled challengingly. 'I tell you what, I'll be generous and let you lead.'

Something clenched in his gut. Did it show on his face? She looked at him keenly.

'Well?'

'I haven't seen the scans,' he said.

'No problem. I'll brief you now. Scans are up there,' she told him, nodding her head at the light box behind him. He turned, and his heart sank. Poor bastard.

'We can't hope to get it all,' he said.

'Almost certainly not. Besides, he's also a little jaundiced, so it's quite likely it's metastasised to his liver already.' She filled him in further on the man's history, his symptoms and probable prognosis, which, even before they got inside him, he knew was appalling. And once in there, might prove to be even worse. The oncology team would obviously be involved, but there was a limit to what they would be able to do if it was as bad as it looked from the scan.

'So—there you are, McEwan. Let's go get some answers—and we can see how good you are, now you're finally here.'

* * *

'Ready when you are,' he heard the anaesthetist say, and Kate—*Ms Burgess*—said something pithy on the lines of being there just as soon as the team had finished organising itself.

Stifling a sigh, he finished scrubbing, dried his hands and gowned up. He'd met women like her before—tough, uncompromising, hard as nails, trying to prove themselves as better than the men they worked with, clawing their way up over the backs of anyone who dared to stand between them and their ultimate goal. Well, tough. He could be uncompromising with the best of them, but that wasn't what he was here for. He was here to test the water, to see if this time he could make it work.

And he could. He could grit his teeth and put up with her nasty sense of humour and her evil little digs about his lack of organisation, and make it work.

He had to. He had a living to earn, a career to reconstruct, and a family to hold together.

And Kate Burgess wasn't about to be given the chance to sabotage that.

He was even better looking than she'd remembered.

Not that she'd been exactly studying him at his interview, but she had noticed, and now, in his scrubs—well, they did things for that solid, muscular frame that should have been illegal.

Not overly tall but too tall for her to look him in the eye without tipping her head back, strongly built, with floppy, tawny brown hair that had a tendency to fall down over his forehead—or did, until he'd scraped it back with those long, powerful-looking fingers and tucked it into a theatre cap—

and curious pale blue eyes that seemed to look right through her and find her wanting.

She felt a twinge of guilt, but it wasn't her fault he'd been late, and she'd hung on as long as possible before removing Jo from her duties when her uncomplaining young SHO already had more than enough to do. And she hadn't really been unkind, she thought, trying to justify her behaviour to herself and knowing that she couldn't. She shouldn't have criticised him like that in public, it was unfair and unethical. Damn. She'd have to apologise, but she'd seen the scans and knew what lay ahead, and she hadn't needed a slack member of the team to deal with at the same time.

Especially not a member she hadn't wanted in the first place, even if he was supposedly a fantastic surgeon.

He had an odd history. He'd been a consultant in a London hospital—only for a year—but then he'd left abruptly and hadn't worked since, apart from a few—a very few—highly temporary locum jobs. And it was now well over eighteen months since he'd given up his consultant's post, but he'd applied for the locum job to cover her registrar's maternity leave here at the Audley Memorial in mid-Suffolk, and the hospital board had welcomed him with open arms.

Not her, though. There were too many unanswered questions, too many potential complications, but there wasn't another candidate to come within miles of him. There was just something about him she didn't trust, something she didn't want in a colleague. He was too guarded, too unforthcoming, and he'd refused to be drawn on his career break, deflecting their questions gently but firmly, and citing personal commitments when they had asked why he wasn't going for a permanent post.

'Maybe one day,' he'd said, and that was that. Current employment law precluded any more searching questions, so they were stuck with what he volunteered. Which was next to zilch.

It was odd, though. Odd that a man whose rise through the ranks had been by all accounts meteoric, and whose disappearance from those ranks had been even faster, should emerge only to take a short-term post. Because her registrar *was* coming back, just the moment she'd had her baby and got her child care sorted.

And the previous hospital had spoken incredibly highly of him without telling her anything in the least revealing. So what was the story?

She didn't know, but she was damned if she was going to ask him again, when he couldn't even get himself organised enough to turn up on time with his ducks in a row for his first day at work. The only thing she was sure of was that she wasn't cutting him any slack. He did his job properly to her satisfaction, or he was out. She had a busy surgical team to run, and she didn't carry passengers, no matter what their personal commitments.

She didn't suffer fools gladly, either, and she wasn't starting with this one, no matter how beautifully put together he might be.

She was finished with all that. So finished that she couldn't imagine why she was even thinking about it.

'In your own time, McEwan,' she snapped. Heading for the table, she picked up the iodine swab and sloshed it liberally over the man's abdomen. Then she looked up and met those disturbing pale blue eyes over the body of Mr Symes.

'Your patient, Mr McEwan.'

Meeting the challenge in her eyes with a quirk of his brow, he stepped up to the table and held out his hand.

'Knife, please.'

He ripped off his gloves, peeled off his gown and ditched it in the bin with his hat, and headed for the changing room, Kate hard on his heels.

Of all the cases to start with, of all the evil twists of fate—

'Have you got a problem?'

As if she cared. He turned his head slowly and met her eyes, too raw to be diplomatic. 'Not as far as I'm aware, but you clearly have. Want to get the assassination over now?'

She frowned, propping up the doorframe and managing to look genuinely puzzled. 'Assassination?'

'You've had nothing good to say to me or about me yet today, and I know you didn't want the board to appoint me, so I don't imagine it's going to be pretty. So, do you want to do this now, or would you rather wait until you have an audience before you give me a blow-by-blow of my inadequacies?'

She coloured interestingly, but she held his gaze, to her credit.

'I'm sorry. I shouldn't have said what I did in public like that, but I was…'

'Angry?'

'Frustrated. I wanted to meet you, introduce you to Steve Symes and his wife, go through the case.'

'Instead of which you gave me a scant glance at the scans and hurled me in at the deep end. Why?'

'Because if you were only half as good as everyone said, I knew you could do it, and I wanted to see for myself how good you really were.'

'Or watch me fail.'

She shook her head. 'Not at all. And I was right to trust you. You did a very good job. I couldn't have done it better myself. Possibly not as well. The graft on his femoral artery was a superb piece of surgery, and I'm glad you were able to do a bowel resection so he doesn't have a stoma, so at least he'll have his leg and his dignity if nothing else. It's just a shame it won't save him.'

'We don't know that. It's only just gone off to Histology for grading,' he said. He wasn't falling for her flattery, and he was more concerned about their patient than scoring points, but she shook her head.

'Come on, James, you're good. You saw that mass, and you felt his liver. You know as well as I do what's going on.'

He swallowed and opened his locker door. 'Yes.' He stripped off his top, pulled on his shirt and waited for her to turn away. Apparently she wasn't going to, so with a slight shrug he dropped his scrub bottoms, kicked them off and reached into his locker for his trousers.

She moved then, he noticed wryly, soft colour flooding her cheeks for the second time as she took a step back and then turned on her heel and squeaked across the corridor in her rubber boots to the female changing room as if the floor was on fire.

Dear God, he was gorgeous.

Seriously hot, she thought as she stripped off her own theatre blues and reached for her clothes. And she was his boss, the woman who was going to have to put up with his weak excuses and his evident lack of organisation for the duration.

Fabulous.

Oh, well, at least he was an excellent surgeon, and anyway, she wasn't about to be distracted by his physical charms. She was immune. Utterly immune. She glanced over her shoulder and got a perfect view through the two open doors as he hauled his trousers up over that taut, muscular bottom in its snug jersey boxers, and she stifled a moan.

Maybe she needed a booster vaccine.

She kept her eyes firmly to herself after that, but it didn't help. She'd seen him now, and it wasn't an image she was likely to forget in a hurry. It didn't help, either, that they then went to the ward and she had to watch everyone falling over themselves to find an excuse to talk to him. Well, the women, anyway. The men were giving him wary looks and reassessing their chances with the nurses they'd been hoping to get lucky with, if she knew anything about ward dynamics.

And he was charm itself, but she noticed with interest that he kept a slight distance without being unfriendly, and she also noticed the reappearance of a wedding ring since they'd finished surgery. They'd be disappointed, she thought, and wondered if that curious twinge she'd felt when she'd seen the ring could possibly be put down to it.

Ridiculous. Of course not. She wasn't interested. She didn't do relationships with work colleagues. With men, full stop. Not any more.

'Right, time for a quick check of yesterday's post-ops and we can go and have some lunch before my clinic this afternoon. It'll give me a chance to fill you in on our schedule,' she said, and took him away from his fan club.

And she wasn't sure if that quiet sigh that eased from his throat as they turned and walked down the ward was one of relief or disappointment.

* * *

'So how was your day, Rory?'

''K, I s'pose.'

'Do anything interesting at school?'

'No. Can I watch cartoons?'

'Sure, but just for a little while, then you need a bath and bed.' James stifled a sigh and gave his son a quick one-armed hug. 'Are you hungry? What did you have to eat?'

Rory shook his head, heading for the sitting room. 'We had fish fingers and chips.'

James frowned. Fish fingers and chips? OK occasionally, and goodness knows he'd resorted to that on numerous occasions over the past eighteen months, but if this was what the childminder was going to give the kids every day for supper he was going to have to say something, and he dreaded it. It had been hard enough to find anyone with space who could take Freya all day and pick Rory up from school and keep him till he finished. The last thing he needed to do was make waves.

'Was Freya all right?'

Rory shrugged uncommunicatively. 'S'pose,' he mumbled, dropping down onto the floor and turning on the television, his back to his father.

James put the kettle on, went back into the sitting room and stared broodingly down at his sleeping daughter, still lying where he'd put her when they'd got in a minute ago, out for the count. She was oblivious to the noise of the cartoon, but she'd been up in the night and she was exhausted—and there were tear stains on her downy cheeks.

Oh, damn. Why? Why him? Why Beth? Why any of them?

He wanted to throw back his head and howl at the moon, but it wouldn't get them anywhere and the kids had enough to deal with without their father going off the rails, so he scooped Freya gently into his arms, carried her up to her bedroom and undressed her, changed her nappy and slid her into her cot without waking her.

He'd bath her in the morning. For now she needed sleep more than anything, and he needed to spend some time with Rory and brush up on a few things for work, then phone the childminder and talk to her about their diet.

And then he could go to bed.

'So how was your new registrar?'

Kate gave her father a fleeting smile. 'Oh, very good—if you don't count the fact that he was an hour late because he'd failed to send a vital form back to HR.'

'Oops,' her mother said softly from the Aga. She stirred the gravy thoughtfully and cast her daughter a searching look. 'Will you forgive him?'

'Not if it happens again,' she retorted, and then sighed. And of course her parents both noticed.

'So what's the problem with him?'

'I have no idea,' she said quietly, her thoughts troubled. 'Family problems, I think. Personal commitments, he described them as at his interview, but he looked tired today as if he'd been up all night.' As well as drop-dead gorgeous.

'Married?'

'I don't know. We can't ask that sort of thing any longer, but…he has a ring,' she said slowly, for some reason holding back on saying yes because she just felt, somehow, that he wasn't married. Not any more. So—what, then? Divorced? Widowed? Divorced, most likely. Sharing custody. A messy divorce, then—the sort of divorce that had led children to this house and her parents over and over again, to be loved and cared for and put back together again until things were a little straighter at home.

If they ever were. Sometimes it just didn't happen.

'Sounds as if there's a story there,' her father said, handing her a plate laden with tender slices of roast chicken and crunchy golden roasties. He pushed the bowl of steaming Brussels sprouts towards her and stuck a spoon in it.

'Oh, I'm sure there is,' she said, toughening up. 'There's always a story, but I don't want to hear it. He shouldn't have taken the job if he couldn't hold it down. His personal life is nothing to do with me, and I don't want it affecting his work. If he can't keep it sorted, he shouldn't be there.'

'I think that sounds a little harsh,' her mother said, sitting down at the other end of the battered old farmhouse table and setting the gravy jug down in the middle. 'I know you don't want to get involved, and I realise he has to do his job, but surely, if there was some mix-up?'

'He didn't send in the right forms. If he does that with a patient, fails to get the paperwork in order, then tests could get missed and results disappear and people could die.'

'I'm sure he'll be aware of that,' her father put in, which earned him a look that he returned evenly until finally she sighed and smiled and gave a tiny nod of concession.

'Yes. Yes, of course he's aware of it. And he's a brilliant surgeon—fantastic. Neat, quick, decisive—he'll be a real asset. I'm not surprised he was a consultant. God only knows what he's doing as a locum registrar.'

'Holding his family together, perhaps?' her mother suggested softly, and Kate felt a stab of guilt.

Was that what James was doing? Holding his family together?

'Then why not say so?'

'Maybe he's a very private man. Maybe he doesn't want to talk about it. Maybe it's messy and embarrassing or just too hurtful to talk about.'

Like her own divorce.

'Maybe,' she conceded, wondering.

'Cut him a little slack, Kate,' her mother advised. 'Give him time—for the children.'

'We don't even know if there are any children,' she pointed out, but she had to bear it in mind, just in case. She couldn't do anything else, because without her parents, who weren't her parents at all, her life would have been very, very different.

'OK, enough about work. How are you guys? Good day?' she said, handing over the conversation to them. Piling the hot, steaming sprouts onto her plate, she poured over the gravy, picked up her knife and fork and started eating as she listened.

He couldn't sleep.

Apart from the fact that he was kicking himself about the bloody form he'd failed to send in, and the heart-rending interview he'd had with Amanda Symes at her sleeping husband's bedside in the high-dependency unit, there was an image of Kate Burgess in her underwear burned onto his retinas, and every time he closed his eyes he could see it, the smooth skin, the sleek curves—and the ugly, wicked scar that snaked over her ribs.

Surgery. Emergency surgery. A thoracotomy?

Looked like it. He'd dragged his eyes away and finished dressing, and then for the rest of the day he'd felt as if his eyes were burning through her clothes. It was a wonder they hadn't caught fire, and he was stunned at himself.

He hadn't looked at another woman since he'd met Beth eight years ago, and he sure as hell didn't need to be fantasising about a woman who wouldn't be out of place in *The Taming of the Shrew*!

No. That was unfair. She'd been right, he should have been there on time with all his boxes ticked. It had been unprofessional, and all the excuses in the world wouldn't make it right.

He swallowed the disappointment that he'd let himself down at the first hurdle. Stupid, stupid oversight. And now, of course, she'd be worried that his paperwork wouldn't be up to scratch.

Well, he'd just have to prove her wrong.

He rolled to his side, punched his pillow and rammed it into the side of his neck, then closed his eyes and saw her again. Naked, except for a few scraps of outrageous underwear and a scar that raised more questions than he wanted answers for.

He was on time the next day, but he looked exhausted.

'How's Stephen Symes?' he asked without preamble, and Kate gave him a searching look and smiled pointedly. 'Good morning.'

'Morning. Sorry,' he mumbled. 'So—Mr Symes?'

'He's back on the ward. He spent the night in HDU but he's OK. The histology's back.'

'Bad?' he asked, and she nodded.

'As it can be,' she told him, and the muscle in his jaw tensed. 'It's a grade three, dirty margins—but we knew that at the time, knew we hadn't got all of it. And the histology indicates that it's aggressive, which is borne out by the liver involvement. So it's Stage IV, as we suspected, and we're talking palliative care. Oncology is onto it.'

'Have you spoken to him, or have they? Told him the news?'

'I thought I might let you do that, as you were the one who operated, and as you spoke to his wife yesterday afternoon. I gather from what she said over the weekend that he was the sort of man who wanted all the answers, and when I spoke to her yesterday after you'd discussed the operation with her she told me he'd want to know the truth.'

'How much of it?'

'Not enough to terrify him,' she said, and something flickered in his eyes. 'Just give him the bare bones, and let the oncologist and onco nurse fill him in on the treatment plan and likely course of events. It's their department, not ours.'

'Is his wife here?'

'Not at the moment. She's gone home—she's coming back shortly.'

'Right. Where is he?'

'Bay two, bed four.'

'Notes?'

She arched a brow and handed him the notes, and he took them and glanced at the results, then shut the file and walked away, pausing to wash his hands and rub them with alcohol gel. He took his ring off to wash it before putting it back on, and she was relieved to see that he was fastidious and she didn't need to keep an eye on that, at least.

But she couldn't stop herself keeping an eye on that ring, and she found herself wondering about him again as he replaced it and twisted it round, just once, thoughtfully, before squaring his shoulders and heading towards their patient.

Crazy. She was wondering altogether too much. She watched him walk up to Mr Symes and pull the curtain a little to screen him from his neighbour, then shake his hand, his face serious. He didn't let go of his hand, though, didn't distance himself as he delivered the news, and she stood there and watched the man's face through the gap in the curtain as it all sank in, and wished it could have been different.

He spent several minutes with him, and then came back to the nursing station, his eyes bleak.

'OK?' she asked, and he nodded.

'It wasn't exactly unexpected. He said he'd had an idea that was what it was, so he wasn't expecting a miracle, but that sort of news is always a shock. I think he just needs time for it to sink in before we tell him much more, or it'll go straight over his head.'

'We can go through it again. I'm sure we'll have to, to answer all his questions.' She sighed. 'It's such a waste. If only he'd reported his symptoms sooner, before it'd had time to metastasise.'

'But you don't, do you?' he said flatly. 'Even if you know—even if you're a doctor—you just assume it's IBS or something you ate and it becomes part of life to have an irregular bowel pattern, because nobody wants to believe that it can be anything sinister.'

There was something odd about his voice, and that bleak look in his eyes was even bleaker. He sucked in a breath and straightened up, his eyes going blank. 'So—we need to contact the onco nurse and the oncologist, get some treatment set up for him asap.'

'I've done it,' she told him. 'The oncologist is on his way down. I'd like you to speak to him and tell him exactly what you've told Mr Symes, and I'd like you to be there when he talks to them. His wife's on her way. I've asked her to join us, so she can be involved in the discussion.'

He nodded. 'Good. Thanks.'

He was about to say something when she caught sight of the oncologist striding down the ward towards them, and she opened her mouth to greet him and was cut off by his exclamation.

'James? What the hell are you doing here?' he asked, shaking his hand warmly.

It was the first time she'd seen James smile with his eyes, and the change was astonishing. 'Working—locuming, as of yesterday. How are you? I'd forgotten you'd moved up here. How's it going?'

'Fine, great. What about you? I haven't seen you for ages, not since—well, last September, I suppose. I didn't realise you'd left London now as well.'

'No,' he said, the smile fading. 'We're OK, Guy. We're getting there. We've moved to be closer to my mother and my in-laws.'

'And Freya?'

The smile was back, softer this time. 'Freya's fine. Doing well, and Rory's started school. We ought to meet up.'

'That would be good. Come over some time. Sarah would love to see them again. So—what have you got for me, Kate?' he asked, getting back to business, and Kate saw James's smile retreat once more as she spoke.

'CA bowel—terminal ileum, caecum and attachment to the rear wall over the right femoral artery. We did a hemicolectomy to remove the obstruction and James dissected out what he could, but it's only a short-term fix to give him some symptomatic relief. He's almost certainly got liver mets. We're waiting for some blood results to confirm that but he's jaundiced and there are small but palpable masses in the liver.'

Guy winced and gave James a keen look. 'Ouch.'

James shrugged, and Kate picked up swirling undercurrents. She'd known there was something, but now Guy was watching James closely and those curious blue eyes were flat and shuttered. 'It was a bit tricky, but he's come through it well, considering,' he said gruffly. 'I've told him what to expect within reason and without putting the fear of God into him, but you'll need to go over it and dot the Is and cross the Ts.'

'Shall we go and talk to him, then, in a few minutes? I'd like to see the notes first.'

'Of course. I'll be back in a minute.' James handed over the notes and excused himself, and Guy flicked through them and sighed.

'Tough one, this, for him to start with.'

'So it seems,' she said, fishing, but before he could say any more they were interrupted by a soft voice.

'Dr Burgess?'

She turned and saw Amanda Symes standing at her side, her eyes strained and red-rimmed and her face pale. 'Mrs Symes— thank you for joining us. This is Dr Croft. He's the oncologist who's going to be taking over your husband's care. He's going to go through things with you both.'

'Oh. Right. Um—and the other doctor? James—Dr McEwan, was it? I'd like him there, he was so kind to me yesterday.'

'I'm right here,' James said, appearing again from nowhere and smiling gently at her. 'Hello again, Amanda. Shall we go into the office?'

It wouldn't have been so bad if he hadn't known exactly what was in store for them.

As it was, he was only too painfully aware of every twist

and turn in the road ahead, but Guy led the discussion and he really didn't need to have anything to do with it.

Except, of course, he felt involved for all manner of unsound and unprofessional reasons. He put them on one side and forced himself to concentrate on this case, this man, this spouse whose life was about to be turned upside down, this family that was going to be torn apart by fate.

But not his. Not this time.

CHAPTER TWO

THE next few days were tough.

Rory was OK-ish and coped with the change of routine just like he'd coped with everything the last year and a half had thrown at him, with quiet stoicism, but Freya was slower to settle. She'd spent time with the childminder before he'd started the job, to give her time to get used to her, but the new regime of long days and early starts was making her tired and grizzly.

At least the food issue wasn't an issue, really. Helen had given them fish fingers and chips at Rory's suggestion because they'd gone home via the park to feed the ducks and had needed something quick, and she'd been meaning to ask him for a list of things the children liked. And the next night they'd had roast chicken with lots of veg, which he was more than happy about.

But on Wednesday night, as they'd arranged, his mother picked them up from the childminder straight after school and took them home with her to her little flat because he was on call, and that unsettled Freya even more.

'She just wouldn't go to bed,' his mother told him unhappily on the phone the next day. 'I know it's difficult, but I think it would be better if I came to you in future—familiar territory and all that. It makes the bedtime routine more normal and I can't bear it when she's so unhappy.'

All of which made absolute sense—except his spare bedroom was a storeroom at the moment, and it would take a mammoth effort to clear it.

An effort he didn't have the time or inclination to make, but he knew he had to stop stalling and get to grips with the house, so he ordered a little skip on Friday and in the evening systematically went through all the stuff in the room—old paperwork, things from his student days, some of Beth's things that he'd kept—nothing important, nothing sentimental or relevant or remotely useful, just things he hadn't got round to dealing with before the move—and first thing in the morning, he carted them downstairs and threw them all out.

He was heading towards the skip with the last armful when Kate walked up the drive towards him.

Hell. He stopped, horribly conscious of the state of the house, the task he was undertaking and the mess he was in, but she just smiled and waggled his mobile phone at him.

'You left this on my desk. I found it this morning when I popped in to check up on something. It's got several missed calls, so I thought you might want it. I would have called you, but HR said it was the only number registered to you, and I didn't want to call your mother and worry her. They gave me your address.'

I'll just bet they did, he thought, wondering how she'd sweet-talked that out of them, and what else she'd managed to get them to yield up. Not that it mattered.

'Thanks.' He dropped the last of Beth's possessions into the skip with a quiet sigh and took the phone from her, then added, 'Want a cup of tea?'

He didn't know why he was asking, except she'd gone out

of her way to return his phone, he was dying of thirst and he'd decided he didn't actually care whether she was impressed or not by where he lived. It was none of her damn business.

'That would be lovely,' she said, looking slightly surprised. 'Thank you.'

He ran a mental eye over the inside of the fridge and wondered if he had milk. Probably. And maybe even teabags. And perhaps at a pinch he might even find a biscuit...

He led her through to the kitchen and put the kettle on, wincing at the dishes piled in the sink, but she stood in front of them, looking out of the window, and totally ignored the mess.

'What a lovely garden.'

'It is—or it will be when I get round to doing anything with it. That's one of the reasons I bought the house. Well, that and the fact that it's got four bedrooms, so my mother can come and stay when I get the spare room straight—if I ever get round to that, either. I have a hell of a to-do list!' he added wryly.

She turned and studied him. 'Is that what you're doing with the skip?' she asked, and he busied himself with the mugs so he didn't have to meet her eye.

'Yes. I've been lazy—used the spare room as a glory hole. Thought it was time for a sort out.'

She didn't need to know what he'd been sorting out, and he didn't volunteer anything further. He carefully avoided telling her why his mother needed to stay as well, or anything else about his child-care arrangements. It was none of her business, and if he possibly could, he'd like to keep it that way. Keep all of it that way, except of course she couldn't fail to notice the absence of a woman's touch. He'd never been good at the stage-setting part of houses, unlike Beth, who'd been fantastic at it and would have had the place licked into shape in no time.

And she certainly wouldn't have had dishes stacked in the sink! Oh, well, he'd get a dishwasher just as soon as the kitchen was refitted, but one thing at a time, and washing up never hurt anyone.

The kettle boiled and he poured the water onto the last two teabags in their mugs, poked them with a spoon and lifted them out. 'Milk?'

'Yes, please.'

'I might even have some biscuits,' he said, rummaging in the cupboard, but she shook her head, and her hair, long and loose today so it hung down round her shoulders, swung and bounced and gleamed in the sunshine and did something odd to his gut.

'I don't need a biscuit, thanks. The tea's fine.'

'OK.' He straightened up, and suddenly there was a curious tension in the air between them, a strange electric current that drew his eyes to hers and made his heart beat just a little harder. He needed space—more than an arm's length between them—so he didn't feel tempted to reach out and see if that hair felt as soft and smooth and heavy as it looked.

'Um, come through to the sitting room,' he said, holding the door for her, and led her to yet another scene of chaos.

Rory was lying on his stomach in front of the television, watching cartoons again, Freya was sitting in a pool of Lego bricks and constructing a rather wobbly tower, and the cushions were all pulled off the sofa and propped up against it to make tunnels and hidey-holes. And there was an ominous smell.

He closed his eyes and sighed.

'Have you guys trashed this place enough?' he asked

mildly, putting his cup down and picking up two of the cushions. and Freya ran over to him and pulled them back off the sofa.

'Daddy, no!' she wailed, even though she hadn't been playing with them at the time. 'House!'

He stopped and sat down, scooping her onto his lap. 'I'm sorry, sweetheart. It's just we need to sit down. Look, this is Kate—she's a friend of mine,' he said, wondering if that was pushing it too far, but Freya looked up at Kate and studied her dubiously, Rory swivelled round and sat up and stared, and Kate, to her credit, ignored the cushions, sat on the floor in front of the sofa and stared right back, a smile playing round her lips.

'Hi, guys,' she said softly. 'Did you make a den? I used to do that.'

'Did you get into trouble?' Rory asked soberly.

The smile became rueful. 'I don't remember, so probably not very much. So—who are you guys?'

'I'm Rory,' Rory said, 'and she's Freya. Dad, she needs her nappy changed.'

'I know,' he said, wrinkling his nose and smiling at Kate, a little bemused by the change in her. 'Sorry. Will you excuse us for a minute?'

'Go right ahead,' she said.

He took Freya out and dealt with the nappy and found her and Rory a cracker, which was the closest thing he could get to a biscuit, and some juice, then went back in to find Kate sitting cross-legged on the floor next to Rory in the midst of all the toys, watching cartoons with every appearance of enjoyment. Bizarre.

He raised a brow, and she laughed a little self-consciously and got up and perched on the edge of the sofa.

'Sorry. I like cartoons,' she confessed, and he rolled his eyes and handed her her tea with a reluctant smile, trying not to think about how that laugh and the faint touch of colour accompanying it had softened her features and brought warmth and something else to those surprisingly lovely caramel eyes.

Something that made him think of things he'd put out of his mind a lifetime ago.

'I should drink it fairly fast, it's getting cold,' he said hastily, and dropped into the other corner of the sofa, wincing as he hit the unprotected springs. 'Sweetheart, can we please have the cushions back for a bit?' he asked Freya, and she nodded absently, her attention drawn by the television.

He sorted them out before she changed her mind, and Kate settled back into the cushions and smiled at him. 'This is a lovely house.'

He gave a stunned laugh. 'Well, it probably will be, but it's a bit of a project. I wanted something we could make ours and, let's face it, there's plenty of potential here. Not much else, though.'

'Oh, it'll be beautiful. It's got fabulous high ceilings. I love Edwardian houses.'

'I've never had one before. I'm beginning to think it might have been a mistake.'

'Really?'

He laughed. 'No, not really. I'm sure it'll be lovely eventually.'

She tipped her head on one side and regarded him thoughtfully. 'It must be a bit of handful having two very young children and a new job and trying to do the house up all at once,' she said softly.

And he thought, She doesn't know the half of it, and I'm damned if I'm telling her.

'It's OK,' he said, reluctant to suggest for a moment that it was anything other than plain sailing. She didn't need to know the number of times this last week he'd come *that* close to throwing in the towel. Except, of course, he couldn't afford to. Eighteen months out of work had left him sailing pretty close to the wind. His investments had buffered them, and he was careful, but the house was going to take a substantial sum to fix it up and, besides, it was time to get their lives back on track.

And if they were really lucky, they'd all survive the experience…

He hadn't said 'we'.

Not once, unless he'd been referring to the children as well. 'I bought the house—when I get it straight—if I ever get round to it. I've been lazy.'

As if there wasn't a Mrs McEwan.

There was certainly no evidence of a woman's touch in the rundown and desperately outdated house, although the furniture obviously came from better times and there was no lack of homeliness or warmth. And the children were lovely once they opened up, especially Rory. Funny and charming and sweetly innocent, and the spitting image of his father. Freya had been just as charming, but more wary of her.

James had been a little wary, too, she thought as she drove home. As if he hadn't really wanted to invite her in, but hadn't felt there was a choice. He'd almost been defiant about it— *this is me, take it or leave it.*

And his blunt honesty had sneaked under her guard.

Her mother was just unloading shopping from the car when she turned into the drive, so instead of going into her own home in part of the converted barn on the other side of the farmyard, she went over and helped her mother carry the food into the big farmhouse kitchen, the dogs trailing hopefully at their heels.

'Been at work?' her mother asked, and she gave a little smile as she put the bags down on the table and patted the dogs.

'Sort of. Earlier. I've just been to see James—he left his phone behind last night and I dropped it in to him.'

Her mother straightened up from the fridge. 'And?' she asked, getting straight to the point.

'He's got two little children—Rory, who's about five, I suppose, and Freya, who must be coming up for eighteen months or so. Toddling about and starting to talk, and definitely got a personality.'

'Don't sound so surprised. Babies are born with personality.'

And she knew that, of course, and over the years she'd seen enough small children in her mother's care to be well aware, but somehow Freya's personality had taken her by surprise. She was so *stubborn*, such a determined little thing, and very much her daddy's girl.

But, then, that wouldn't be surprising, would it, if she didn't *have* a mother in her life?

'And the mum?' her mother asked, as if reading her mind, and Kate shrugged thoughtfully.

'I don't know if there is one.'

She tutted softly, her face pleating in a sad frown. 'Poor little mites.'

'Mmm.'

She thought of the dishes in the sink, the chaos in the sitting room, the garden that still, even in December, had garden furniture and toys lying out in it, and she thought of the dark shadows round his eyes and the weary grey pallor of his skin, as if all the sun had gone out of his life.

And then she thought of the way she'd greeted him on his first morning, less than a week ago, and felt a wash of guilt.

'Don't beat yourself up,' her mother advised, reading her mind again. 'You didn't know, and if he chose not to tell you…'

'But he still hasn't, so I still don't really know. She might just have been out shopping. They might be bone idle and useless at housework.'

But she knew that wasn't the answer.

Fortunately, because he had the rest of the weekend off, James was able to get the bedroom sorted out so his mother could come and stay when he was next on call.

Well, sorted was perhaps a little generous, he thought, staring gloomily at it late on Sunday night. He'd given it a quick coat of paint over the top of the existing wallpaper just to freshen it up, but apart from that he hadn't had time to do more than wipe down the woodwork with a damp cloth, vacuum the elderly carpet and make the bed.

Oh, well, he thought tiredly, at least the bed was a comfortable one. They'd had it in London, bought it so their friends and relations could come to stay at a time when things had been looking good.

He switched off the light, walked out and closed the door.

He'd done all he could for now. It needed some serious attention in the future, but it would do for the short term and get over the problem of unsettling the children.

He dropped them off with the childminder on Monday morning, and walked into the ward to discover that Stephen Symes had started to feel pins and needles in his right hand and was feeling dizzy.

It could have been anything—maybe a few tiny clots from the femoral artery repair he'd had to do—but he had a hideous sinking feeling that it was more metastases, this time in his brain.

Well, at least it would be quick, he thought heavily as they did the ward round and checked their post-ops who'd been in over the weekend. They were all doing well, and while he was waiting for Mr Symes to come back from the scanner, he discharged two of the patients and filled out the paperwork. By the time he'd finished, Mr Symes was back, so he went to talk to him.

'Is there any news?' he asked James instantly, and he shook his head.

'Not that I know. They'll contact us later. You got missed in the ward round so I thought I'd come and check up on you—how's the tummy?' he asked.

'A bit tender, but much better than it was. I've stopped feeling sick and things are starting to go through me again, so I suppose I should look on the bright side, but it's a bit hard with everything else caving in all around me.'

'I'm sure. I'm glad it's made you more comfortable, though. That's good. Mind if I have a look?'

He shook his head, so James turned back the bedclothes and examined the wound. Neat, clean, healing well, and looking on the bright side, as he'd said, his bowel symptoms were relieved for now. Not so the liver. The yellowish tinge to his skin was a little worse, and the whites of his eyes were also starting to show the effects of the bilirubin in his system.

And then there were the neurological symptoms…

'Will Dr Croft be coming to give me the results of the scan, do you know?' the man asked as James covered him again.

'I expect so. I'll ask him to keep me informed.' He paused

and met his eyes. 'It may be nothing, you know. Don't borrow trouble.'

He smiled wearily. 'No. I've been feeling a little light-headed and woozy off and on for weeks. I thought it was because I wasn't keeping much down or eating very much, but I doubt it. Is there any way I can get the results before my wife gets here for visiting at three?'

'I'll chase it up,' James promised, and, leaving him, he went back to the nursing station and got the switchboard to page Guy.

'Any news on Symes?'

'Yes—I was just coming up. Not good, I'm afraid.'

James sighed. He'd thought as much. 'OK. I'll be on the ward.'

'I'll come and find you before I tell him, show you the photos.'

'Cheers.'

Guy took a few minutes, and in that time James chased up some lab results for another patient and requested a nasogastric tube to aspirate a nauseous patient in under observation for query appendix with a very atypical presentation.

He'd just finished writing up the notes when Guy arrived at his elbow and snapped the film onto the light box. 'There you go. Three of the little bastards,' he said softly, pointing out the small white blobs on the plate.

'Will you do anything?'

He shrugged. 'We could give him radiotherapy, but it needs a head mask to hold him in the same position every time and he struggled with the scanner, apparently. A bit claustrophobic—and the mask is worse, as you know. I'll talk to him, see how he feels. He might think it's not worth the hassle, given the odds. I don't need to elaborate, I take it?'

James shook his head and took a nice, slow breath. 'No. It's all utterly familiar.'

Guy cocked his head on one side and studied him searchingly, so that he felt like a bug under a microscope. 'Are you OK with this? Do you want me to handle it alone?'

'No, and no,' James said frankly, and Guy gave a wry, understanding smile and laughed without humour.

'Let's go and tell him, then.'

'I gather Stephen Symes has got brain mets.'

'Yup.'

Kate studied him for anything further, but there wasn't a flicker. He could have been utterly indifferent, but she just knew he wasn't. 'How sad,' she prompted.

There was a flicker then, a tiny one, gone before she could analyse it. 'You think? In his shoes I'd welcome it. At least it'll get it over with.'

Kate sighed inwardly. She'd have to see if she could get some information out of Guy. So far he'd been disappointingly unforthcoming, but she didn't want to come right out and ask James where his wife was and what had happened to her. She had a horrible feeling she knew the answer.

'Clinic this afternoon,' she said, changing the subject. 'There's a teenage girl with vomiting, weight loss and a small mass in the upper abdomen. I was going to see her, but I'm busy with follow-ups on patients I really want to see, and I'm feeling generous, so I'll let you have her—see what you make of it. You might want to do a gastroscopy. And if you have any difficulties—if you feel I need to see her…'

'Is that likely?' he asked, and she had to convince herself to let go. She liked to see the kids herself.

'Probably not. But just in case. There's also a patient

with Crohn's who might need surgery tomorrow, and I'll give you a few others. I know you're more than capable. Have you had lunch?'

He shook his head.

'Neither have I. Why don't we go down now and grab something on our way to the clinic?'

For a moment she thought he was going to refuse, but then he shrugged. 'Sure,' he said, and scrubbed his hand through his hair. It fell straight back down again, and she had a sudden urge to lift it out of the way, to run her fingers through it and see if it felt as soft and silky as it looked.

Crazy. He was a colleague. Her locum registrar—which made her his boss, for goodness' sake! She couldn't go fantasising about running her fingers through his hair.

Or kissing that firm, unsmiling mouth, or any of the hundred and one other inappropriate things she'd been thinking about ever since Saturday morning when she'd seen him in his lovely, rundown house in those washed-out charcoal jeans and a pale blue jumper that had matched his eyes and looked soft enough to stroke.

She glanced again at his hair as they sat down with their sandwiches and coffee, and smiled.

'Is the job getting to you, or were you painting over the weekend?'

He frowned, then before she could stop herself she lifted a hand to his hair and tested the offending lock between finger and thumb. Oh, yes. Soft. So soft, except for the crisp little strands of white.

'Ah. Painting,' he said with a crooked grin, making her heart lurch, and she snatched her hand back.

No! She couldn't let him get to her. She didn't do relationships, and she certainly didn't do casual sex, so there was no point torturing herself with the thought. No matter how suddenly appealing…

'I needed to get the spare room sorted so my mother can stay when I'm on call,' he went on, fingering the strand she'd touched. 'Hence the skip, as you so rightly surmised, and the paint—which I seem to be wearing. I'm not exactly gifted in the DIY department. Well, the house department generally,' he qualified, torturing her again with that reluctant grin. 'Give me a nice messy RTA victim with massive internal injuries over decorating any day.'

She chuckled. 'I love decorating,' she confessed. 'I find it relaxing and therapeutic.'

One eyebrow quirked sceptically. 'Probably because you're better at it than I am. I get paint everywhere except where I'm meant to, and I always get the ceiling colour on the walls and the walls on the ceiling.'

'Remind me not to let you loose on my barn, then,' she said with a laugh. 'I don't need paint splodged on my beams.'

'You've got a barn?'

She nodded. 'Well, part of one. On my parents' farm,' she added, wondering why she was revealing things about herself that she wouldn't normally discuss at work, but for some reason her tongue kept on rolling. 'We converted it and split it into two units, and I've got one half and the other half is a holiday cottage-cum-guest accommodation.'

He cocked his head on one side. 'Do you know, I would have put you in a modern penthouse flat,' he said thoughtfully, and she found a smile from somewhere.

'Been there, done that,' she said lightly, trying not think about it, but while they were on the subject, she wondered yet again why he was in a house that needed so much work when she would have expected him to own something much better.

Something, for instance, that went with the furniture in his house and the BMW on the drive.

Unless his wife had left him and taken him to the cleaners? She pushed a bit.

'I would have put you in a rather smart executive house in a quiet leafy avenue,' she returned, testing him out, and his face went carefully blank.

'Been there, done that,' he said in an echo of her words, and she decided not to push any more for now. There'd be plenty of time to find out more about him—and, anyway, it was irrelevant. On a need-to-know basis, she didn't.

So she'd keep her nose out, and so long as he turned up and did his job, his private life was none of her business.

Just like hers was none of his.

Tracy Farthing, the fifteen-year-old with the vomiting and weight loss, was interesting. His first reaction had been, Oh, no, not another one. But once he'd looked at her, his gut instinct made him consider less obvious possibilities.

He examined her, and could feel a diffuse but very definite mass in her abdomen, just where her stomach would be. He helped her up off the examination couch and sat down again opposite her and her mother, running the various possibilities through his head.

'So—what do you think, Doctor?' her mother asked, looking worried.

As well she might.

'I'm not sure. I want to run some tests, take some bloods and see if anything significant emerges from the results. We know from the urine sample you brought in that you're not pregnant.'

'Well, of course she's not pregnant!' her mother said indignantly, but he noticed that Tracy's shoulders dropped a fraction, as if she was relieved, and he just smiled.

'Mrs Farthing, it's in no way a value judgement—a pregnancy test is routine in any woman between puberty and the menopause to eliminate the possibility,' he explained, and watched her subside, mollified. 'Having done that, we can then proceed to all the other possibilities.'

And then he noticed the girl's hair. It might have been the way she'd slept on it, or dried it, but it seemed thinner on the left side, more sparse. That wouldn't fit, though, unless—and as he glanced down at the notes, he noticed out of the corner of his eye that her hand had crept up and she was fiddling with it. Her left hand.

'Do you do that a lot?' he asked, and she nodded, looking embarrassed and lowering her hand quickly.

'Oh, she's always fiddling with her hair,' her mother said a little impatiently. 'She's done it for years. Why?'

'Just curious. Tracy, I think I'd like to have a look into your stomach,' he told her. 'There's a very simple procedure called a gastroscopy, where we numb the back of your throat and ask you to swallow a tube that's connected to a special camera, so we can see inside without having to give you an operation. It's painless, a little bit unpleasant and takes about five minutes, but there are no side-effects and it'll give us answers very quickly. I'd like to do it now, if you're willing? It could save an awful lot of time.'

She gave her mother a worried look. 'Mum?'

Her mother shrugged. 'Tracy, it's not my body, I can't tell you what to do.'

'That's rubbish, you tell me all the time!'

'But not about something like this.'

'Well, what would you do?'

She smiled worriedly. 'I'd listen to the doctor,' she replied. 'If he thinks it's a good idea, I'd believe him. Besides, you want to know what's going on, don't you?'

She hesitated another moment, then nodded. 'All right, then,' she agreed. 'If you're sure you need to do it?'

'I need to—and it's really not that bad.'

'How do you know? Have you ever had it done?'

He shook his head and smiled. 'No, but I've done it to lots of people and, believe me, they'd tell me if it was too dreadful. They don't usually hold back.'

She gave a faint smile and nodded. 'OK. But can you stop if I really don't like it?'

'Yes, of course I can, but it's very quick. Probably less than five minutes. Two?'

'Promise?'

He gave a little chuckle and shook his head. 'No, I can't promise, but I wouldn't lie to you.'

'Would you have it done?'

'Oh, yes. No hesitation. It's very straightforward, and it doesn't hurt. It just feels a bit odd and makes you retch a bit. If you could go back to the waiting room, I'll make the necessary arrangements and then let you know if we'll be able to do it today.'

She hesitated again, then nodded, and he gave a silent sigh of relief as they left and reached for the phone. 'Kate, I've just seen Tracy Farthing. Can I have a word about her?'

'Sure. I'm free for a second. Come on in.'

He went next door to her consulting room and perched on the desk. 'I'm guessing wildly, but her hair's a bit sparse and she fiddles with it. Her mother says she's done it for years.'

Kate frowned curiously. 'A trichobezoar? I don't think

I've ever seen one—unless you count the hairballs my mother's cat used to bring up!'

He chuckled. 'No, I haven't either. Certainly I've never seen one large enough to cause this kind of obstruction. I'd like to do a gastroscopy—what are the chances this afternoon?'

'Ring Endoscopy and tell them you're bringing her up—unless you want me to do it?'

He laughed softly. 'You really don't trust me with her, do you?' he murmured, and was fascinated to see a little brush of colour on her cheeks.

'Of course I trust you. I'm just not used to being able to delegate to such an extent,' she said, trying to talk her way out of it. 'Are you going to sedate her or use the anaesthetic spray?'

'Spray,' he said firmly, having done both and having assessed that Tracy was basically calm, reasonable and likely to be compliant. He much preferred working with an alert, co-operative patient so he could explain things as he went along.

'In which case there shouldn't be a problem,' Kate said. 'Ring them now. I'll carry on working through the clinic patients—but feel free to call me if you want a second opinion.'

'Kate, I'm fine,' he said firmly, and he took Tracy and her mother up to the endoscopy suite, talked them through the procedure and showed Mrs Farthing out, then sprayed the back of Tracy's throat and quickly and easily passed the tube down into her stomach.

Her full, distended, hair-filled stomach.

'Well, I've got your answer,' he told her when he'd removed the tube and called her mother into the room, showing them the tiny bit of hair he'd teased off.

'What is it?'

'Hair,' he said. 'You've probably been pulling it out and swallowing it in your sleep. The trouble is the hair gets in a knot, then it can't move on, and it just gets bigger and bigger—'

'Oh, gross,' Tracy said, wiping her mouth on a tissue and gagging slightly. 'That's disgusting.'

'It's one of those strange things that people do for no very good or known reason. It's called trichophagia, which means literally hair-eating, and it often starts in childhood and can persist into adulthood totally subconsciously—you probably do it in your sleep.'

She pulled a horrified face and looked near to tears. 'I want it out.'

'That's the plan, because it's not doing you any good at all. You need to stay here in the waiting area until your throat's feeling normal again and you can swallow properly, Tracy, then come back to the clinic and see me and I'll run through what we're going to do.'

He left them with the endoscopy nursing staff and went back to the clinic, tapping on Kate's door. She looked up and smiled.

'Perfect timing, I was just about to call my next patient. So—what do you know?'

'Spot on. It's massive. I want to admit her as a matter of urgency and remove it before she starts to suffer with gastric bleeding from the abrasion.'

'I agree. We're operating tomorrow. I've got a couple of patients I've seen today who are much more urgent than their referrals suggest, one of them the Crohn's case I was telling you about, so stick her on the list with them and we'll just have to hope we aren't too busy overnight.'

'I'll tell her to come in later today, then,' he said. 'What do you want me to do now? More outpatients?'

She frowned. 'Actually, no, I'd like you to talk to Mrs Symes. She's waiting for you.'

He felt his heart sink, and swallowed. 'OK. I'll talk to her now, and then see Tracy when she's back down.'

He walked along the corridor to the waiting area, saw Amanda Symes staring out of the window blankly and went over to her.

'Amanda?'

She turned, her hand on her chest, and gave him a very half-hearted smile. 'You made me jump, I was miles away.'

In hell, he thought, judging by the look of her. 'I'm sorry. Come on, let's go and have a chat. Fancy a cup of tea?'

'Have you got time, James? I don't want to be a bother.'

'It's no bother, I could murder for one. I haven't had time to stop yet this afternoon.'

He paused by the reception desk. 'Any chance of two cups of tea in my consulting room?' he asked, and the receptionist nodded.

'I'll get them brought through to you,' she said, reaching for the phone, and he took Amanda to his room and sat her down.

'So—how can I help?' he asked gently.

'I don't know that you can. I don't know that anyone can, but— Oh, James, I don't want him to die,' she said, and started to cry.

CHAPTER THREE

THERE was nothing he could do except let her talk, and he did that, for as long as he felt it was productive, but when they started going round in circles he stopped her.

'You really need to talk to the oncology nurse. She's trained to deal with this situation, and she has lots of practical things she can offer to help you both. I'm not trying to get rid of you, but I'm not really the best person to help you now. I've done all I can to make things better for him, unless he needs further bowel surgery in the future, but the onco nurse has an amazing range of things she can offer to make things easier. Talk to her. Make friends with her, and with the Macmillan or Marie Curie nurses. They'll look after you, Amanda. They won't let you deal with this alone.'

Her face crumpled again, and she made a valiant effort to control the threatening tears. 'I am, though. I feel so alone. It's crazy. It's as if in a way he's already gone, and I feel so *angry* with him for leaving me.'

He nodded, aching for her, knowing that distancing himself was impossible because he was with her every step of the way. 'That's the start of the grieving process,' he explained, his voice a little gruff. 'Accept it for what it is, and just remember that, however hard it gets, it's not going to go on for ever, and you can get through it, and you're not alone. And although I can't really help you, if you want to talk to me again, at any time, I'll always find time to see you.'

He showed her out, a little surprised when she hugged him, and then shut the door and leaned on it.

I feel so alone. It's crazy. It's as if in a way he's already gone.

He swallowed hard, trying not to get sucked in by the memories, and after a moment he eased himself away from the door and sat down again.

Poor woman. Poor man. Poor all of them. He hauled in a steadying breath, closed his eyes for a moment and then picked up the receiver.

'Is Tracy Farthing back in the clinic?'

'How did the Farthings react?'

James ran his hand round the back of his neck and frowned. 'OK. She's gone home to get some things and she's coming back in this evening.'

'Have you set up a psych referral?'

He shook his head. 'I was going to ask you about that. I don't know what your protocols are here, but she'll need counselling and psychotherapy or she'll just do it again. I think there's a lot going on in her life that her mother doesn't know about.'

Kate laughed. 'She's a teenager. Of course there is. I'll sort Psych out. What about Amanda Symes?' she added, and watched a shadow pass over his face.

'I've referred her to the onco nurse and the Macmillan or Marie Curie people and given her a couple of websites to look up.'

'Good. Thank you. Right, we're on call tonight. I'm just

going to shoot up to the ward and check things are OK for tomorrow, then I'm going home to read up on the hairball op. Can you give me a ring if anything comes in that I need to know about? Jo's here—she'll help you.'

He nodded, and she thought she could see tension around his eyes. 'Will do,' he said, and, picking up the notes for Tracy Farthing, he headed out of the door.

She followed slowly, contemplated staying around, and told herself not to be ridiculous. He was paid to do a job. Let him do it—he was more than capable. And if he couldn't manage it because of his family commitments, then he'd have to go, kids or no kids. She couldn't carry him.

James headed up to the paediatric ward, wondering what the night would bring and if he'd manage to get through it without his children waking and refusing to let him out of the door if his pager went.

Hopefully not.

He introduced himself to the charge nurse, then told her, 'I've got a fifteen-year-old coming in for tomorrow's list. She's got a trichobezoar—a hairball in her stomach—and we're going to remove it in the morning.'

She blinked and widened her already wide eyes. 'Wow. That's unusual.'

'Absolutely. I've never done one and neither has Kate. Hopefully she'll be fine and won't need to go to ITU, but she'll need careful monitoring in case she gets gastric bleeding because of the abrasion of the hair on her stomach lining.'

The charge nurse nodded. 'We'll make sure she's got qualified cover for the first twenty-four hours. What about a psychiatric referral?'

'Kate was contacting them.'

'OK. I'll follow it up. They can come and chat to her this evening, reassure her about the surgery.'

'Thanks. She's called Tracy Farthing—oh, and mum's a bit unaware of her social life, I think. She looked relieved about the negative pregnancy test, but the mother was indignant.'

She laughed. 'They always are. Don't worry, we'll look after her. I'll put her with a girl who's having a knee op tomorrow. They can keep each other company in our teenagers' section.'

'Thanks. Jo's around overnight, and I'm on call so I'll be in and out. Page us if you need to, and I'll pop in and make sure she's OK at some point.'

'Cheers. I'm Trina, by the way. I'll be on again tomorrow morning so, if I don't see you later, I'll see you then.'

'Great. Cheers, Trina.'

He walked away, wondering if that had really been an invitation in her wide and welcoming eyes, and if so how he felt about it.

Stunned, he decided. It was so long since he'd been in the marketplace he'd forgotten what it was like. Horrible, from what he could remember, but then for some reason an image of Kate flashed into his mind and took him by surprise.

No fluttering lashes there, no wide-open soft baby blues, just sharp shards of toffee slicing through him assessingly.

Not always, though. Sometimes—like when she'd been in his house, watching cartoons with Rory, or after he'd painted the room and she'd lifted her hand and touched his hair—then her eyes had been soft and warm and—

No. She was his boss, and he'd do well to remember it. And, please, God, nothing would happen tonight to shake her faith in his ability or make her question giving him the job…

* * *

'Freya, I have to go, darling.'

'No!'

'Yes. I'm sorry, sweetheart. We'll do something lovely at the weekend.'

'Not go!' she sobbed, clinging to him, and he handed her, screaming, to his mother, ran down the stairs and walked out of the door, blinking back the tears that had come from nowhere.

Her wails followed him out to the car, and he shut the door and started the engine to drown out the heart-rending sound. She'd get used to it. The trouble was they'd had too much time together, and she wasn't used to him leaving her. She'd stop crying soon. She'd probably stopped already.

'Penny for them.'

He scrubbed a hand through his hair and sighed. 'Oh, nothing, Jo. Freya was a bit miserable when I left her,' he confessed.

'Freya?'

'My daughter.'

'Can't your wife comfort her?'

He looked at the SHO, her eyes red with exhaustion as they snatched a much-needed coffee in a quiet moment, and for some reason—tiredness, probably—he told her about Beth. Nothing much. Very little, really. The bare bones, but it was enough.

'That's such a shame. I'm really sorry.'

'Yeah. Thanks. My mother's with them, so it's not like leaving them with a stranger.'

'But kids are funny. She'll get used to it, though.'

His pager sounded, then Jo's, and he sighed and glanced at the little screen. 'Finish your coffee. I'll go down to A and E and see what we've got. I'll page you if we need Theatre.'

He made his way to A and E, and found Tom Whittaker, the consultant on duty, in majors. He was working on a young man, inserting a second IV line, and James glanced at the monitor and frowned at the blood pressure.

'Blunt abdominal trauma—we haven't done a DPL but he's hypovolaemic. I think you've got time to get him upstairs, but not much else. He's crashing. Apparently he's been kicked.'

'Charming. Right, let's get him stabilised and we'll take him into Theatre. I'll page Jo and get her primed.'

'The police'll want to talk to him.'

'Well, we'll have to make sure we keep him alive, then,' he said drily.

They set up fluids and then sent him off on his way to Theatre. Following the trolley, James paused at the door and turned to Tom.

'Are you OK?' he asked, looking at him keenly, and Tom gave a wry smile.

'Ah, I just hate violence. Bit too close to home.'

James tilted his head questioningly, and Tom went on, 'I was stabbed here by a patient last year—in April. I nearly bled out. It's still a little fresh in the mind.'

A year ago last April. The month his own life had fallen apart. It was, as Tom said, still a little fresh in the mind.

'I can understand that,' he said. 'Thanks for your help. I'll keep you posted on this one.'

'Do that.'

It was touch and go, once they'd opened him up, but there was no point in calling Kate. She wouldn't have got there in time, and anyway he and Jo could manage.

Just about.

Jo's surgical skills were slight, but she was a fast learner and she did as she was told without question, which meant he could rely on her. Always an asset in a crisis.

He removed the man's spleen, stitched the tear in his liver and put him back together again. And then, once their patient was stable and everything was back under control, he phoned Tom and told him, then went home, crept in through the door and fell into bed, exhausted.

Three hours. That was all. Three hours, before he had to be up again and on the way out. At least his mother was here, so he didn't have to get the children ready first.

Three and a half, then.

Oh, joy.

'Kate, I'm sorry, I'm going to be late. Can you start without me and I'll get in as soon as possible?'

She swung round and propped her feet on her desk, rolled her eyes and thought, *Here we go.* 'Do I have a choice?'

She heard him sigh. 'Yes, you have a choice. If you can't cope without me, I'll come in now. But I'd rather not. It would be…difficult,' he said after a pause.

Difficult? 'Oh, I can *cope*, McEwan,' she said, wondering if her voice sounded as bitter as she thought it did. 'I just don't see why I should be expected to without any kind of explanation. Is it a problem with the children?' she added, softening her voice, and he sighed.

'Yes, and no. It's…complicated. Don't worry, I'll deal with it. I shouldn't be too late.'

'James, it's always complicated,' she said, exasperated by his refusal to open up. 'We've got a busy morning—Tracy Farthing, for starters. Your patient. I need you here doing your job. Whatever's wrong, if it's not a matter of life or death, just sort it and get here asap.'

She hung up the phone with a bang and turned, to find Jo standing right behind her.

'He's going to be late. I'll need you to help me.'

'Oh. I wondered. His daughter was playing up in the night. It's such a shame about his wife. He's a lovely guy.'

'Jo, don't gossip,' she said, sounding like a shrew again for the second time in as many minutes, but Jo was used to her, she could cope, and Kate swung her feet to the floor and stood up, putting James and his wife—whatever had happened to her—right out of her mind. 'Right, let's have a look at what came in last night. Were you busy? I was half expecting a call.'

'Oh, no, we coped fine. It was quite quiet in a frantic sort of way. James was amazing—well, apart from being hassled. He's a brilliant surgeon.'

Kate said nothing, not really caring how amazing and brilliant he was if he couldn't manage to get here, still irritated by his refusal to tell her what was going on, and Jo went on, 'There was a straightforward appendix, and a couple of admissions for observation and assessment—oh, and we had to open up Mr Reason again. His drain had dislodged— he'd pulled on it by accident a couple of days ago, he said, and he'd developed an abscess. And then there was a ruptured spleen and liver laceration from a fight. He'd been kicked in the abdomen and it was a bit tricky, but James was fantastic. He's fine, doing well, but the police want to talk to him once he's up to it, to see if he can identify his attacker.'

Oh, Lord. She felt a surge of adrenaline but pulled her mind back into focus. 'Good. Right. We'll start with a look round them, then the pre-ops, and then if James still hasn't turned up, I'll go and talk to Tracy Farthing in Paeds.'

She didn't want to hear that James had been amazing and brilliant and fantastic, she was feeling antsy about the police and the fight victim, and generally she was irritated. Whatever had happened to her nice, orderly existence? It was all so messy and complicated now, and until her registrar had gone off on maternity leave, it had all been going so well.

Trust a man to come in and throw a spanner in the works, she thought crossly, and stalked off down the ward, leaving Jo and Liz, the staff nurse, to follow with the notes.

She didn't want to think about the fight, so she thought about James, instead, and how he'd talked to Jo. *Such a shame about his wife.* That was another annoying thing. How could he? How could he just open up and talk to her SHO when she'd been deliberately kept in ignorance?

'Morning, Mr Reason. I'm sorry to hear you had to go back to Theatre in the night. How are you feeling now?'

Tracy Farthing's operation went smoothly, no thanks to the start of his day, with Freya clinging to him like a limpet and his mother's rather tepid attempts at removing her.

Saying things like, 'Oh, poor little thing, she doesn't want you to go, James. You can't do this to her, she needs you, she's lost her mummy,' really didn't help. At all. Any of them.

Particularly not Rory, who was the only one of the two to remember his mother and even he didn't talk about her any more.

'This is nothing to do with Beth,' he said firmly. 'This is about a little girl who doesn't want her father to leave her, but she needs to learn that I have to go to work, and that I come back at the end of the day. I'm hardly the world's first lone parent. Millions of people do it. It's simple.'

But it didn't feel simple, and in the end his mother had refused to be left with her while she was so upset, in case she couldn't get her to stay with the childminder.

'You know I'm supposed to be going to see my sister, James—she's expecting me. She's seeing the consultant today, and she wants me there. Please, don't leave me with them,' she pleaded, and so he took the children to the child-minder himself, prised Freya off him again and handed her to Helen, took Rory straight to school since it was now so late, gave him a brief, hard hug at the gates and arrived at the hospital just before nine.

In time to start the list with Kate, in a taut silence broken only by terse remarks relating to Tracy's operation. Then, once they'd finished and he'd closed, he straightened up and met her eyes and knew he was in trouble again.

Deep, deep trouble—and he really didn't give a damn.

They walked out of Theatre, leaving the team to clean and restock it ready for the Crohn's patient, and he watched as she dropped into one of the plastic chairs in the lounge area and fixed him with a look that could have melted a hole in the wall.

Tough. He walked over to the coffee-machine, poured two cups and went back, handing her one and lowering himself into a seat at right angles to her.

'Come on, then, spit it out.'

'I don't think I've got anything to say,' she told him bluntly.

'I think you have, though—starting with an apology, and following up with an explanation, because I don't think you can expect me to support you when things go wrong if I'm kept in the dark like a bloody mushroom! What's going on, James? I need to know.'

He ran a hand round the back of his neck and sighed, conceding her point. 'Fair enough,' he said tiredly. 'But not here. Not now.'

'Why not?'

He met her eyes defiantly, his impotence at the situation

turning suddenly to anger, boiling up inside him like lava and threatening to spill over and destroy everything it touched. He clamped it back under control and bit out, 'Because if you're going to want me to spill my guts, I'm doing it on my turf, on my terms.'

'Tonight, then? At yours?'

'Won't your husband mind?'

She looked startled for a second. 'I don't have a husband,' she retorted after a breathless pause. 'My time's my own.'

He nodded curtly, storing that bit of information. 'All right, then, tonight, if you insist. Come about eight. No. Make that eight-thirty—let the kids get off to sleep.'

'Fine. Will you have eaten?'

'What's that got to do with anything?'

She shrugged. 'I probably won't have done. I can bring something—Chinese? Indian?'

Oh, Lord. A curry. He hadn't had a curry in ages. He so nearly said no, anger getting the better of him, because he knew perfectly well that she was just doing it to soften him up and make it harder for him to kick her out before she was ready, but then he thought of the pitiful contents of his fridge and his self-control went belly up. So what if he went a little over budget? It was damn well about time. 'Indian,' he said decisively, and let his taste buds decide. 'Lamb balti, Bombay potatoes, pilau rice and a peshwari naan. And beer. I'll order it in,' he added, trying to repossess the moral high ground, but she wasn't having any.

'No,' she said, holding up her hand. 'I'll bring the food. This meeting's my idea. And in return I want my questions answered. Properly. The truth, the whole truth, et cetera. You owe me that.'

She drained her coffee and stood up, walked out to the

sinks and started scrubbing for the next case, leaving him to follow in his own time, his anger tempered by the curiously interesting fact that there was no Mr Burgess…

Oh, God, he was turning her into a dragon.

She wasn't a dragon. She was usually reasonable, caring, accommodating—it was only James who did this to her, and it was driving her nuts.

Was that why she was dithering and vacillating over her wardrobe? For a *meeting*?

'Oh, good grief, you are ridiculous!' she told herself. Pulling on a clean pair of jeans and a pretty V-necked jumper over a little vest top, she gave herself a last look in the mirror, ran her fingers through her hair and decided to leave it down and headed for the door.

She looked fine. It wasn't a date.

It wasn't.

Freya was in bed and asleep by seven. She'd obviously worn herself out the night before, and the childminder had taken her and her own child to feed the ducks in the afternoon on the way to pick Rory up from school, so she'd been out in the fresh air and been running around.

Thank heavens, because frankly he'd had enough emotional turmoil with his tiny daughter for today and he could have done without Kate coming round and giving him the third degree tonight.

Curry or no curry.

He went into the kitchen and found it spotless. His mother had obviously cleared everything away before she'd left, and the sitting room, similarly, was tidy, except for a little random chaos generated before bedtime. He breathed a sigh of relief, because he really didn't have the energy to get a duster out, never mind the vacuum.

He glanced in the mirror and wondered if he should change, then gave a soft grunt of derision.

Into what? A power suit?

This was his house, his territory—his home, for goodness' sake. What he wore in it was his own affair, and he was perfectly certain that Kate would have her say no matter what he had on.

And, anyway, it was too late. His jeans would have to do. Her headlights swept across the front of the house, then cut out, and taking a deep breath, he ran downstairs and opened the front door as she got out of the car. Keep it civil, he told himself, but he couldn't quite get himself to dredge up a smile.

'Hi.'

'Hi.' She looked up and smiled tentatively, brown paper carrier in hand, and he held open the door and beckoned her in, mesmerised by the waterfall of dark, glossy hair that tumbled down her back and jerked him suddenly and comprehensively out of the sexual coma he'd been in since Beth's diagnosis.

'I couldn't remember what you said—lamb balti and some kind of naan bread and rice, so I just got that and a few other bits and pieces, and a chicken passanda.'

He forced himself to concentrate on her words, and unglued his tongue from the roof of his mouth. 'Fantastic. It smells amazing. I haven't had a curry for ages. Come on in, let me take your coat.'

She slid it off and handed it to him, and then he nearly dropped the curry because she was wearing snug jeans that cuddled her lush little bottom like a lover and a pretty, pale pink jumper with a low V-neck, and if it hadn't been for the little frill of white lace across it he would have had a perfect view down her cleavage.

Thank heavens for vest tops, he thought fervently, and went into the kitchen with the carrier bag and pulled the containers out. Several of them. Wow! 'Table or knees?' he asked.

'Table, I think,' she said with a slightly embarrassed smile. 'There's quite a lot. I got a bit carried away.'

He chuckled, but it sounded a bit rusty. All he could think about was her getting carried away, and his mind was going into meltdown. He plonked the things onto a tray and led her through to the dining room.

She'd probably over-ordered by about fifty per cent, she thought, going back to the passanda and rice for another helping and ripping a bit off the peshwari naan just for good measure.

Still, he was diving into it as if he hadn't eaten in ages, and maybe he hadn't. But they hadn't talked yet, and possibly he was stalling. She let him eat, though, until even he was slowing down, and then she decided to call a halt.

Putting her fork down, she pushed her plate away and met his eyes across the mess of containers and spilt rice and scraps of naan.

'Talk to me,' she said softly. 'I don't bite.'

'Like hell,' he muttered, but he put his own fork down and reached for his beer, turning the glass round while he studied it thoughtfully, a frown pleating his brow.

Then he looked straight at her. 'OK, what do you want to know?'

'I have no idea, since I have no idea what it is I don't know. I know you have children, I know you've spent a long time away from work, I know that at interview you were cagey in the extreme about your domestic situation, but I have no idea what that situation really is. I don't even know,' she went on evenly, 'if your wife is still alive.'

He put the glass down very carefully and met her eyes again, his breath easing out in a shaky sigh. 'No. She died last year, in August. She had cancer.'

Oh, God. She'd thought as much, but hearing it…

She didn't bother with platitudes. Her regrets or otherwise were irrelevant. So she waited, and after a moment, he went on.

'It all started in April. Beth was six months pregnant with Freya, and she wasn't feeling great. She'd been suffering from constipation, and thought it was the iron tablets. She hadn't told me anything, but then one morning she vomited and started passing blood. She got a taxi to the hospital, got herself admitted and by the time I knew about it she'd had a load of tests and was waiting for the results.'

'She didn't tell you?'

'No. Because she knew—she was a doctor, and she wasn't stupid—and she didn't know where to start. Anyway, the results came back. She had a tumour in her ascending colon, but because she'd ignored her symptoms for months— possibly even years—it had spread to her liver. By the end she had mets in her spine and ribs, and finally her brain.'

Like Steve Symes, she thought, and wondered if that explained his terse and rather crabby behaviour on the first day. Of all the dreadful coincidences…

'She died at the end of August, three months after Freya was born.'

He lifted the glass and drained it, then sat forward, picking up his fork and prodding the food on his plate, his expression bleak. 'It was tough. I was angry with her, because she'd ignored her symptoms until it was too late to do anything about the pregnancy, but even if she'd had it terminated, she wouldn't have survived. She might have had longer with Rory, but Freya would have been dead and that would have destroyed her. As it was they had a few good weeks together before she started to really go downhill.'

He put the fork down and stood up abruptly.

'Coffee?'

'Thank you, that would be lovely,' she said, feeling a little surreal, and when he headed out of the door towards the kitchen, she sat there for a few seconds, gathering her thoughts. He'd said his wife had been a doctor, and she remembered something else he'd said to her, after he'd told Steve Symes the news. *Even if you know—even if you're a doctor—you just assume it's IBS or something you ate, because nobody wants to believe that it can be anything sinister.*

His remark made sense now, she thought, and suddenly the way he'd dealt so sensitively and sympathetically with the whole family made absolute sense as well. He'd been great with them. As if he had known exactly what they were going through. Which, of course, he did. And by making him the lead on the operation, she'd hurled him in at the deep end of his worst nightmare.

Oh, if only she'd known…

With a soft sigh, she got to her feet and started to clear the table.

It was a mess—bits of this and that—but enough to make another meal. She took the tray of containers through to the kitchen and put it down. 'Shall I put these onto a plate for you to have tomorrow?' she suggested, and then she looked up and realised he was standing motionless, staring out of the window into the black night.

She could see his face reflected in the glass, drawn and expressionless, and she shrugged and left him to it, finding a plate in a cupboard, piling the remains of the food onto it and covering it with a bowl.

It was ridiculously easy to find space for it in the fridge. It was all but empty, and she wondered when he found time to shop for food.

Not your problem, she told herself, and scraped the plates into an empty container before putting them by the sink.

'Dishwasher?' she said, but he didn't move.

'James? Do you want me to go? Or just go to hell?'

He made a strangled sound that could have been a laugh, and turned towards her. 'Now, there's an idea,' he said, and then smiled a little crookedly. 'However, since I need your goodwill—just leave them there, I'll do them later. We haven't got a dishwasher yet. It's on the list, like everything else. Do you mind instant? I think the real coffee's probably on its last legs. I forgot to put it back in the freezer.'

'Instant's fine,' she agreed. 'Where's your bin?'

'Under the sink,' he said, taking the empty containers and ditching them. 'You don't have to do that.'

'Well, someone does, and you're making coffee. Have you got a cloth? The table looks as if we've had a food fight.'

His mouth kicked up at one side, and he wrung a cloth out under the hot tap and handed it to her. 'You can't hurt the table, it's sealed,' he said, and turned back to the kettle, dismissing her—but not for long. She hadn't had all her answers yet, not by a long way, and she wasn't going until she had…

CHAPTER FOUR

IT WASN'T over, of course. She'd barely started. He knew that, and they went through to the sitting room with their coffee, settled down at opposite ends of the sofa and he waited for her to get back into her stride.

It didn't take many seconds.

'Talk to me about your child-care arrangements,' she said bluntly, and he felt his right eyebrow climb, but of course she didn't back down, just fixed him with that implacable gaze and waded on in.

'Yes, I know, I shouldn't ask, but since I had to cover for you this morning, and as I'm sure it won't be the last time, I need to know that you're doing everything you can and that there's nothing else that could be done to make things smoother.'

'You have shares in child care?' he said, with only a trace of sarcasm, but she caught it, of course, and gave him one of her patented looks with those toffee-shard eyes.

'You want my help? Work with me here, McEwan,' she said firmly, and he gave up. At least talking about his problems kept his mind off his libido.

'I have a childminder. I drop the children off on my way to work, she takes Rory to school, keeps Freya all day, fetches

Rory from school and I pick them up from her at the end of my day. When I'm on call, my mother stays here and does it for me.'

At the moment, but he wasn't sure what the hell he was going to do after the fiasco this morning.

'So what went wrong today?'

'Freya,' he said reluctantly. 'She didn't want to me to go to work in the night—the pager woke her. We sleep with the doors open, and she heard it go off, heard me talking and getting dressed, and kicked off. And then this morning she wouldn't let me go, my mother said she was too upset to go to the childminder and she couldn't look after her—her sister's not well and she had to go to visit her in hospital in Cambridge—and, well, she wouldn't back me up. Said Freya didn't want me to go, poor little thing, she'd lost her mummy—well, I do know that, I have noticed,' he said, unable to kept the sarcasm out of his voice, 'but in fact she hasn't lost her mother, she's never really had one, she just didn't want me to leave. We've had a couple of bad experiences—an au pair who was a living nightmare, and a crèche that she hated. I thought the childminder might be the answer, once she got used to the idea.'

'Hence taking a locum job?'

He nodded. 'A short-term contract, just to see if I can make the arrangements work this time. I thought I could, with my mother to rely on as back-up, but…' He broke off with a short sigh, staring down into his coffee, but there were no answers in the bottom of the mug, just the dregs of an indifferent brew that frankly he couldn't be bothered with.

He put the mug down on the coffee-table and sat back, searching her eyes for clues to her reaction, but there were none.

'So that's my sorry, pathetic little tale. Does it answer all your questions?'

God, he sounded so bitter, but he couldn't deal with this. He had so much on his plate that Kate analysing his child-care arrangements was just the last straw. He knew they were inadequate. He knew it wasn't ideal, but what the hell else was he supposed to do?

'It sounds as if you've done everything you can to smooth the way for them. I'm sorry I was hard on you, but—'

'The patients have to come first? I know that.'

'Actually, no. Without a doctor to treat them, the patients don't get better, so the doctor has to come first. Which is why I wanted to know if there was anything that could be improved, to make your arrangements more robust.'

'Short of fostering them out or giving them up for adoption, probably not,' he said with an attempt at humour, but her face paled and she drew back.

He frowned at her thoughtfully. 'Did I say something?'

She looked away, shook her head and put her cup down with a clatter on the table, her usually rock-steady composure obviously unsettled. 'No. No, of course not. It's late, I'd better go. Um—thank you for telling me all of this. I realise it can't have been easy.'

'Kate? I was joking. There's no way on God's earth I'd give my kids up. Although it has been suggested.'

Her eyes flew back to his, wide with shock. 'Why? Who by?'

He shrugged. 'Friends? My mother, even, at one point. I think she still believes it would be better for them in some ways.'

'No!'

So much emphasis on such a tiny little word, scarcely audible over the indrawn breath, and yet...

'No?'

'Not unless…'

'Unless?'

She gave a tiny shrug. 'Unless there's no choice. Adoption isn't always bad. Sometimes it can be a miracle. But—not just because you don't want them.'

'But I do want them,' he assured her, 'so it won't ever happen. Not while there's breath in my body. I love my kids to bits, and I'd go to the ends of the earth before I'd give them up or let anything bad happen to them.'

Her shoulders dropped, and she smiled and stood up, tugging her jumper down unconsciously, still ill at ease. 'Good. Right, now I have to go—things to do before tomorrow. And I'm sorry I was so hard on you. If there's anything I can do—you know, if you have a problem, if things don't go right…'

'I thought I had to sort it unless it was a matter of life or death?' he said wryly, and he saw something very human and rather desperate going on in her eyes. As if she was torn between her role as his boss and the warm and caring woman he was beginning to realise she hid under that crisp exterior.

'It's only an offer of help in an emergency, so don't push it,' she said, dragging back control of the situation, and he smiled and held her coat for her.

'Thank you—and thank you for the curry,' he said quietly. 'It was a good idea, and I really enjoyed it.'

She looked up, her eyes soft, and her lips curved up in a warm, genuine smile. 'My pleasure. Your turn next time.'

There was going to be one?

'Done,' he said quickly before she changed her mind.

'And next time I promise I won't bully you.'

He grinned and reached for the doorknob. 'I'll hold you to

that,' he said, and for a second he found himself contemplating kissing her goodnight.

Not a proper kiss. Just a peck on the cheek, a brush of his lips against that soft, baby-smooth skin.

He yanked the door open, held it until she'd started her car, then shut it firmly. It was cold out there, a definite nip in the breeze, but inside him a fire was starting to smoulder, and it was the last thing he needed.

He cleared up the kitchen, washed up the dishes and went to bed.

There was ice on the windscreen the following morning, and he had to scrape it off before he could take the kids to the childminder, and then he got caught in the traffic and so, of course, he was late.

Kate was going to skin him, and all the ground he'd made up the night before would be down the pan.

Oh, well, he thought, at least he'd find out how sincere she'd been about helping him through this, but when he arrived on the ward he found her talking to the police, and she turned to him with relief in her eyes, his lateness apparently not the first thing on her mind.

'Ah, Mr McEwan. The police would like to talk to you about Peter Graham, the man in the fight.'

'Oh, right. Sure.'

'If you're happy without me?' she said, and left them as if she couldn't get away quick enough. Things to do?

Or something else?

He spoke to the police, told them what little he knew, accompanied them while they spoke to the patient and then sent them away when the patient became distressed.

'Did they get what they needed?' Kate asked, her eyes not

nearly as casual as her voice, and he looked at her keenly. She looked away. Interesting.

'Not really. He says he doesn't know the man.'

She lifted her head and met his eyes again briefly. 'Well, maybe he doesn't.'

'I think he does. I think we should keep a close eye on his visitors. One of them might be trying to stop him talking.'

She stood up abruptly. 'Well, you do whatever you feel is necessary. Would you go and check on Tracy Farthing, please? I've got a meeting,' she said, and walked away, leaving him even more convinced there was something going on.

He could always suggest a curry at her place and grill her like a kipper until he found out the truth. He had a feeling it was something to do with the scar on her ribs, but short of coming out and asking her, which would mean admitting he'd looked across into the female changing room on the first day and spied on her, there was no way he was going to find out until she was ready to tell him.

He had a feeling hell would freeze first.

And talking of freezing, he ought to buy some de-icer on the way home, ready for the morning. Tomorrow, if he was late, he might not get off so lightly.

It was bitterly cold.

She drove home at the end of the day, wishing Peter Graham had never come onto their ward, wishing it had happened when someone else had been on take so she didn't have to be reminded, and she looked at the dark windows of her little home and felt a shiver of something cold run over her.

The lights were on in the farmhouse. She could go in there,

sit down with them, spend the evening with them. Her father would walk her back later and stay while she put the lights on without needing to be asked, but she couldn't keep relying on them. She had to deal with this on her own. It had been years. It was time she got over it.

She got out of the car and the security lights on her barn came on, flooding the yard with light.

There. She could see the door, she didn't need her parents to hold her hand. She let herself in, turned on all the lights and went up to her bedroom, changed into jeans and a jumper and went back down. Her fridge, although better filled than James's, was still a little on the scanty side and nothing much appealed to her.

She poured herself a glass of wine, sat down and flicked on the television, then her mobile phone rang. She glanced at the screen and saw James's name. 'What's the problem?' she said without preamble, and she heard him sigh.

'Kate, I'm sorry to trouble you but my boiler doesn't seem to be working. I thought it was a bit cold this morning, but tonight it's just plain off and there's a smell of gas in the kitchen.'

'Turn the gas off!' she said quickly, and he gave a weary chuckle.

'Don't panic, Kate, I'm not a total dunce. Can you give me the name of a plumber?'

'No, but I know someone who can,' she said with a smile, ridiculously pleased that he'd phoned her, stupidly happy to hear his voice again after—oh, an hour? 'You need Fliss Whittaker, Tom's wife. You know, from A and E?'

'I know Tom. His wife's a plumber?'

His voice sounded incredulous, and she laughed. 'No. Well, she's all sorts. She's a nurse, but she's done property developing and she knows everyone in the trade. She'll sort you out if anyone can. I'll text you their number.'

'They won't mind you giving it to me?'

'Of course not. They're lovely. If they don't answer, leave a message and they'll ring you back. They'll be putting the kids to bed. They have a lot. I forget how many, but six or seven.'

'Good grief,' he said faintly, and she laughed.

'Quite. The only person who thinks it's reasonable is my mother. Let me know how you get on. And if they can't help you, if you need anything else, ring me back. It doesn't matter how late it is.'

'I will. Thanks.'

She returned the phone carefully to its cradle, then stared at it for a moment before she realised she had a silly smile on her face.

Stupid. And, anyway, it was nothing to smile about. He had two small children in a house without heating, the weather had taken a turn for the worse and the forecast was awful, and this close to Christmas she doubted he'd get anything done unless it was a very simple repair.

Oh, well. He could always go and stay with his mother, she thought, and then remembered the trouble they were having over the business of Freya going to the childminder, and realised that that was unlikely to work.

Not your worry, she reminded herself fiercely, and turned her attention back to the television.

'Sorry, mate, it's shot. You need a new boiler, and half of your radiators are on the point of giving up. You need a complete new system to bring it up to scratch, and there's no way I can get to you now until after Christmas, and that means putting someone else off.'

James stared at the plumber in disbelief, then stabbed his

fingers through his hair and let out a huff of desperation. 'Um—what about a temporary fix?' he asked, clutching at straws, but Joe shook his head.

'Sorry. Can't do it. The burner's gone and it's such an old boiler it's a miracle it's still going. I wouldn't fix it even if I could. It's a miracle it hasn't blown up.'

James felt sick. Sick with the thought of what could have happened, sick with the fact that yet again he was going to have to fall back on his mother's rapidly diminishing good-will—and even if they went to hers, it could only be for one night. There was no way they could stay there for weeks.

'Can I light the gas fire in the sitting room?' he asked, clutching at straws. 'Or use the cooker?'

'Yeah, sure. I'll cap the supply to the boiler so you'll still have gas, but what about hot water?'

'Um—there's an immersion heater.'

'Is it working?'

He shrugged. 'Probably not, knowing my luck. I've never tried it.'

The plumber smiled. 'Let's have a look.'

He opened the door and pulled out a pile of towels and sheets, and Joe stuck his head in and turned on the switch. 'Let's have a cup of tea while that heats up and I cap the boiler, and then I can tell you if it's OK,' he said, so James obediently put the kettle on, watched him sort out the gas before they had a crisis. No sooner had he made the tea than Freya started to cry, and he went and lifted her out of her cot and brought her down to the kitchen to meet the plumber.

'This is Joe,' he said, and Joe grinned at her.

'Hello, love. You look about the same age as my youngest. What's your name?'

'F'eya,' she said, and then suddenly became overwhelmed

and burrowed into her father's neck. He hugged her gently, then met the plumber's eyes.

'Shall we find out the verdict on the immersion heater?' he asked, and they trooped up to the landing and Joe reached his hand in and felt the top of the tank under the old jacket that barely covered it, and shook his head.

'Dead as a dodo. Sorry, James. You haven't got any hot water.'

'Can you change it?'

'I don't know. It's been there so long it might be seized in. I'll try for you, I've got a spare on the van. Give me a minute.'

But it was hopeless. He couldn't free it without risking twisting the fitting out of the thin copper wall of the cylinder, which meant no hot water.

Joy. No heat, no water.

And no home.

He swallowed hard as he shut the door behind the plumber. He'd refused to charge him, which might have been something to do with Rory coming out of his bedroom and telling him he was cold and asking Joe if he could fix it, the hopeful look in his eyes dashed by Joe's reply.

'I'm cold, Daddy,' Rory said now, shivering in his little pyjamas with one foot crossed over the other for warmth as he stood in the chilly hall, and James gathered him into his side and hugged him.

'I know. I'm cold, too. Let's go in the sitting room and light the fire,' he said, and he got their bedding and snuggled them down in the room, then when they were settled he went out to the kitchen and phoned Kate to give her the news.

She was mad.

She had to be mad. They weren't her problem, she kept telling herself crossly as she trekked across the farmyard to the house and let herself in.

Not in any way her problem.

'What's the matter?' her mother asked, shooting her a keen look as she went into the drawing room, and she sat down next to the fire and sighed.

'James,' she said. 'His boiler's broken, the plumber says he needs a new heating system, he's got no hot water and they're huddled round a little fire in the sitting room, freezing. And his mother's got a tiny flat with a very small second bedroom, a four-foot sofa and a very low opinion of his ability to cope.'

'And we've got the barn,' her father added softly.

She sighed. 'Have you got any bookings for it?'

'Only the family coming for Christmas, but that's not for two weeks, and even then I'm sure we can squeeze everyone in. We always do. Why don't you give him a ring?'

'He'll refuse.'

'No, he won't,' her mother said firmly. 'He'll think of the children. I'll go and make the beds up. Andrew, give me a hand. Kate, ring him.'

So they went back to the barn, Kate to her side to ring him, her parents to the other side to turn the heating up from frost protection to full blast and make the beds.

She dialled James's number and he answered on the first ring.

'Hi, Kate. Have you found a boiler fairy in the *Yellow Pages*? I hope so. We're freezing.'

She laughed. 'No. I haven't found a boiler fairy, I've found you a warm house. I want you to come here. You and the children. You know I told you the barn's got a holiday cottage as well as my house? Well, it's empty, and my mother says you're to come.'

'Kate, I can't,' he said with only the slightest hesitation, but he sounded tempted. Very tempted.

'I said you'd say that, and she said you wouldn't, you'd think of the children.'

There was a silence, then a ragged, untidy sigh. 'Kate, I—'

'Don't argue, James,' she told him, softening her voice. 'Pack some clothes, get the children in the car and come over. It's sitting here going begging. It would be ludicrous not to use it.'

'They'll have to let me pay,' he said, and she stifled a smile.

'Whatever,' she said, knowing there wasn't a prayer her parents would take a brass farthing off him. 'Just get here.'

She gave him directions, went next door to help them finish off and her mother looked up from the cot and met her eyes and said, 'Well?'

'He's coming,' she said, and her mother smiled.

'I said he would.'

'He said no. He's talking about paying you.'

'Fiddlesticks!'

'Don't tell him that until the children are safely asleep,' she advised drily, and her father laughed.

'Like that, is he? We'll sort him out. I'm sure he's a sensible man and won't let macho pride get in the way of his children's wellbeing.'

'I don't think he'll let anything get in the way of his children's wellbeing,' she said softly, remembering their conversation about adoption. Grabbing the quilt, she stuffed it into the cover, gave it a hearty flap and tucked it into the cot.

'I've switched on the electric blanket on the double bed, but I'll get hot-water bottles for the children,' her mother said, looking around. 'Oh, and I'll bring over some milk and bread and butter so they can have breakfast. I might even have a box or two of cereal tucked away.'

'I'll go and give her a hand,' her father said, leaving Kate there checking the toiletries in the bathroom and running a duster over the sitting room. Then the lights of James's car swept across the farmyard and she went out and opened his car door and smiled at him.

'OK?'

He nodded, his face defeated. 'Kate, this is so good of you. I feel so guilty, I can't even manage to house my family properly.'

'Don't. Save it, James. You're a good man. You're just in a bad place at the moment. Come on inside and let's get the children tucked up in bed.'

She looked into the back of the car and met the children's eyes, confused and unhappy, and her heart ached for them.

'Come on, kids,' James said softly, and helped Rory out. He reached back in for Freya, and Kate held her hand out to Rory, touched when he put his trustingly into it and leaned against her side.

'Our boiler's broken,' he told her solemnly, and she nodded.

'I know. This one isn't, though. Come on inside, it's lovely and warm. Do you want a nice hot drink?'

'They've had two already to keep them warm. They'll be up and down all night,' James said, emerging from the car with Freya in his arms. Ruffling Rory's hair, he grabbed the bag he'd slung on the floor behind his seat and met her eyes. 'Could you manage this? I've got another one with all our clothes—that's just Freya's emergency bag.'

'Sure.'

She took it and watched him as he lifted another bag out of the boot, locked the car and then turned to her. 'Right. All set?'

'Have you got Mummy's teddy?' Rory asked, and Kate's heart hiccuped.

'It's in the case,' James promised, and then they were ready and she led them inside.

He couldn't believe it.

It was warm. Not just warm, but cosy, and welcoming, and beautifully decorated and furnished in lovely soft neutrals and earth colours, with lots of brick and wood and great thick beams.

It made his house look like—well, like what it was, he thought wretchedly. Shabby and rundown and sad. And cold.

Rory was wide-eyed. 'Wow,' he said softly, looking all around. 'It's huge, Dad!'

'It's only because it's all one room,' Kate said with a smile for his son. 'The kitchen's in here,' she told them, and led them through an open studwork wall into a room the size of his sitting room, with solid wood cabinets and granite worktops and every possible appliance.

Not that you'd know. She had to open the doors to show him where the fridge and freezer and dishwasher were, and it brought it home to him yet again just how far he had to go to sort his house out.

'Ah—here are my parents,' she said, and he turned to see a smiling woman armed with a basket of food. Without hesitation she plonked it down on the worktop and reached for him.

'James, welcome,' she said, enveloping him in a brief, hard hug, patted Freya on the shoulder and said hello, then smiled at his little son, who was stroking the worktop in awe, as well he might. 'You must be Rory. You've had a bit of an adventure, haven't you?' she said calmly, and filled the kettle.

'Our boiler's broken,' he said again. 'Daddy says it's screwed and so are we. What's screwed?'

James nearly choked, but Kate's mother took it in her stride.

'Well—imagine you've got a bit of paper and you twist it up until it's all crumpled. But you can straighten it out again,' she said. She met James's appalled gaze, laughter dancing in the blue depths of her eyes. 'Can't you, James?'

'Absolutely,' he said, his voice sounding strangled.

She straightened up from the fridge. 'There you are—I've put a few essentials in there to start you off, so you can get sorted out in your own time. Kate'll show you where everything is, I just wanted to say hello. I'm Sue, by the way, and this is Andrew—Andrew?'

'I'm here, I was just putting some wood on the fire,' he said, coming through and dusting off his hand before extending it. 'Welcome, James,' he said, and James felt his throat starting to close up.

'Thank you,' he said, his voice suddenly gruff, and he pressed his lips together and eased in a long, slow breath. They were such good people, and without them he didn't know what would have happened to them.

'Right, we'll leave you in peace. There are hot-water bottles in the children's beds, and your electric blanket's on. Kate'll sort you out. We'll see you tomorrow.'

'Let me show you where the bedrooms are so you can get the children off to sleep,' she said as soon as they'd gone, and headed for the stairs, Rory at her side chattering nineteen to the dozen and pretending not to yawn.

'Stay and have a drink with me.'

She looked up into his eyes, on the point of refusing, and saw despair and pride and above all loneliness in them.

'I tell you what, I was just having a glass of wine,' she told him. 'Why don't I go and bring the bottle?'

'My boss, a wino?' he said softly, and she smiled back.

'You don't have to join me if it's against your principles. You can have tea if you like.'

'No way. Go and fetch it. I'll see if your mother's put anything like bread in there. I seem to have forgotten to eat and I could kill for a piece of toast.'

'Me, too. Make lots.'

She went back to her house and retrieved the bottle, then swung back the bookcase and knocked on the communicating door that led from her hall through into the lobby behind the stairs. 'James? Unlock the door!'

She heard the scrape of the key, then he opened the door. 'It's connected,' he said, pointing out the obvious, and she grinned mischievously.

'Ten out of ten. I'll have to get you a pay rise,' she said, pushing past him and heading for the kitchen. 'It was done so that when the family all come down they can take over the barn, but it's usually locked on both sides. Yum, the toast smells good. Here, find a couple of glasses and pour the wine and I'll butter the toast.'

'The family?' he said, clinking glasses. 'You make it sound like there are thousands of them.'

'Oh, there are. Well, not thousands, but lots. My parents foster children. Not so much now, but they have done, for years, and they've grown up and got married and had children and they all come back—and then there are their own children, of course, three of them, and me and my brother.'

He stood and looked at her, and she realised what she'd said and coloured. 'Um—I'm adopted,' she said, and after a long moment he nodded slowly.

'That explains it—your reaction when I said what I did about giving up the children.'

'Oh. Yes. Sorry. I overreacted a bit.'

'No. You were absolutely right. They're my children—my babies. You can't overreact to the idea of losing them—and for the record, I wouldn't ever do it. Here—your wine.'

'Swap,' she said, handing him a plate of hot buttered toast, and they took their little feast through to the sitting room, sat down in front of the glowing woodburner and ate in a silence broken only by the crackle of logs and the distant barking of a dog.

'It's so peaceful here,' he murmured, putting his plate down and settling back into the sofa with a sigh. 'I can't believe I'm sitting here, drinking your wine, eating your food…'

'Not my food,' she corrected with a smile, and he grinned crookedly and stared into the flames.

'Thank you, Kate,' he said softly. 'I don't know what we would have done without you. I can't tell you how grateful I am.'

'Don't be grateful. Just look after your children, get your boiler fixed when you can, and life will sort itself out. It always does, one way or another. You know the saying, when one door closes, another…'

'Slams in your face,' he finished, and gave a quiet snort. 'Or in mine, anyway,' he added.

'James, give it time,' she advised, not really knowing what to say to him but worried that he was expecting too much, too soon. 'You'll get there.'

'I wish I could believe you.' He rested his head back, closed his eyes and sighed. 'It's so nice here. Like a real home. I had one, once. A real home—with love and laughter and the promise of so much still to come. One minute we were sailing along in smug suburban satisfaction, the next it was all gone—like a tatty old jigsaw in a charity shop, with a bit missing.'

Oh, God, she thought, what do I say? What *can* I say? Nothing. So she said nothing, and just waited, giving him time and trying not to cry for him.

'It's not even Beth,' he went on after a long pause. 'It's all the other things. Company. Someone to go to dinner with, or a film or just a walk in the country. Someone to talk to after the kids go to bed, so I don't just go stir crazy and surf the net or go to bed at nine because there's nothing else to do and then lie there alone wondering if I'll ever have a sex life again…'

Oh, yes. She could easily identify with all of that.

Especially, since he'd come into her life, the lying alone and wondering bit.

'I need to go,' she said, getting to her feet and scooping up the dirty plates and her glass. 'Keep the wine, there's only a dribble left. You may as well finish it. Give me a yell if you need anything. I'll leave the door open my side.'

And dumping everything in the kitchen, she headed back next door before she said or did anything stupid.

CHAPTER FIVE

'YOU'RE in early.'

His mouth twisted. 'You mean I'm not late,' he said wryly, and she smiled back, unable to resist his rather rumpled charm.

'Whatever. How are the kids? Did they sleep well?'

'Like logs. They're so confused, they don't know whether they're coming or going, and I think they've just given up trying to make sense of it. Freya didn't make a sound when I handed her over to Helen this morning.'

'She was probably too tired.'

'Probably.' He chuckled and scrubbed a hand round the back of his neck, looking a little awkward suddenly. 'Look, about last night—I'm sorry about the self-pity thing. I didn't mean to wallow all over you like that. I was just at the end of my tether, and you threw me a lifeline and all I could talk about was my tragic and barren existence, so I'm sorry if I came over as ungrateful, because I'm not. I owe you. Big time.'

'It's a pleasure. Right, getting down to business, if you haven't got anything else urgent, could you take a look at Tracy Farthing? I was just about to go up there and check on her. Trina called. She's looking a bit peaky, and complaining of epigastric pain. You might want to have a look at her stomach aspirate and see if there's anything to worry about. Trina said she thought there was evidence of a slight gastric bleed, but that might just be post-op.'

'I'll have a look,' he said, and headed towards the doors, leaving her to do the ward round without him. That was fine, she thought. He could catch up later.

Steve Symes had been discharged to Oncology now, old Mr Reason was doing fine now his abscess had been drained and the only patient apart from Tracy causing them the slightest concern was Peter Graham, the man who'd been kicked in the gut.

He was making slow but good progress, his bowel sounds were returning and they were starting him on free fluids today. Kate normally spent as little time as possible with him, but this morning, for some reason, she hesitated before she walked away.

'This guy who kicked you, Peter,' she said softly. 'Does he bear you a grudge?'

'Nah. Wrong place, wrong time,' he said, but his eyes were shifty and she found herself agreeing with James.

'Well, that's good, because I don't want to send you out there and find you end up in the wrong place at the wrong time again. You might not be so lucky next time.'

Did she imagine it, or did he swallow a little nervously? She left him to it and made her way back to the nursing station with the notes. The senior sister, Ali, was there, and Kate put the notes down and said, 'Can I have a word, Ali?'

'Sure. What's the problem?'

'Peter Graham.'

She frowned. 'What's wrong with him? He was fine earlier.'

'I think he knows the guy.'

'Ah.' Her face cleared. 'So do I. Do you want me to have a word with the police if they come in again?'

'If you catch them. And in the meantime, can you keep an eye out for his visitors in case any of them are dodgy or threatening, or he looks worried while they're here?'

'Of course. I'll give you a head's up if anything odd happens.'

'Tell James,' she said, the fingers of dread plucking at her again. 'He's bigger than me.'

Ali laughed. 'Sure thing. Oh, he rang. He thinks Tracy's got a little gastric bleed. He said, do you want him to do an endoscopy and fix it?'

'That would be a good idea, if he thinks it's bad enough. We don't want to go in again unnecessarily. I'll ring him.'

'Ring who?'

Kate turned round, her hand on her chest, and gave James a mock scowl. 'You made me jump. I was going to call you about Tracy.'

'I've booked a slot in the endoscopy suite for ten to fix it. I'm pretty sure we can do it that way, it's only slight. Want to join me?'

'Could do. I've got a meeting but I know what I'd rather be doing! I'll send my apologies.'

'And we might even get time for coffee,' he murmured. 'I've just realised I didn't manage to get any breakfast.'

She frowned at him. 'And you didn't have supper. You need to eat, James. You'll fade away.'

'Hardly,' he snorted, then cocked his head on one side. 'So—if I need to eat, and you need to eat, is it my turn for the take-away tonight?'

She felt her heart kick up a little speed, and tried for a casual smile. She should say no. She should say—

'Your place or mine?'

He chuckled. 'Rather one and the same, isn't it? Perhaps we'd better make it mine—just in case the kids call out.'

She nodded. 'Whatever. Right, I have to get on. I've got letters to dictate and a whole pile of forms to fill in before I can sneak out and see you do Tracy's gastroscopy.'

'I'm doing it?'

'Sure. Your patient, James, and I'm sure you're quite big enough to do it yourself.'

He tipped his head slightly. 'You're not in the least bit territorial, are you?'

'Not if it means someone else gets to do my work,' she said with a cheeky smile, and, waggling her fingers at him, she headed to her office to wrestle with the hated paperwork.

He got a page that afternoon in his clinic from Ali, and rang her.

'There's a man with Pete Graham and I don't like the look of him,' the ward sister said. 'Nasty—you know what I mean? I don't really want to start anything with him, but Kate said to call you.'

'I'll come. Alert Security, just in case. I don't want him trying anything.'

'Oh. James, he's starting to shout—'

'Call Security. I'm coming,' he said, and ran up to the ward. If the man hit Pete again, so soon after his surgery…

'Get off me!'

'Not a chance,' James said, joining in the fray and pressing the man firmly down onto the end of Pete's bed so the security guard could cuff him. 'Call the police.'

'They're on their way,' Ali said, but he hardly heard her, because Pete was looking pale and shaken, holding his side and—

'Damn, he's going off. He must have hit him. Pete, stay with me. What happened, mate?'

'Hit me,' he whispered threadily.

'Is this the man who hit you before?'

'Brother,' he mumbled, and slid into unconsciousness.

'You're his brother?' he said in disbelief to the man the security guard had wrestled upright.

'He took my girl, all right?'

'I don't care what he did, you don't kick him and nearly kill him and then come in here and have another go! Get him out of the way, please, we're going to Theatre. Ali, let's move!'

They moved. They moved like the wind, wheeling the bed down to Theatre. Someone must have phoned ahead because the doors were standing open and Kate was changed and scrubbing.

'I'll start, you scrub,' she snapped, and took over. By the time he was gowning up, Pete was under and she was ripping opening up the careful layers of sutures that James had put in on Monday night. It hadn't healed much in three days, but by the time she was in, the blood was welling in his abdomen.

'Have we got any blood on order?' he asked, and she nodded.

'Six units on the way up. Ah, it's here. Can you get it in fast, please, someone? Suction, James. I can't see a bloody thing. Thanks.'

'There—the liver, just where I repaired it.' He swore viciously. 'I'd left that lobe, I thought it would heal, but that's gone out the window now, hasn't it? Damn.'

'I might be able to save it. Let me try.'

She did it. To his amazement, she did it, suturing the tear so carefully that he could scarcely see the stitches, and the bleeding stopped.

'Very beautiful. Your great-grandmother would be proud of you,' he said, and she grinned behind her mask, her eyes crinkling up and sending heat shooting through him.

'My great-grandmother would have a fit to think of a girl doing this,' she said. 'But my mother would be proud of me, and that's good enough for me.'

And then he realised her eyes were sparkling, and she blinked and looked away, and he took the instruments out of her hands and took over, closing the wound and replacing all his careful stitches before straightening up and standing back.

'Thank you,' he said to the anaesthetist. Stripping off his gloves, he followed her out and found her slumped in the staffroom, coffee in hand, reading the paper. She put it down when he came in and met his eyes.

'All right?' she said.

'I am. Pete is. What about you?'

She smiled softly. 'I'm fine, but I suppose we should go back to our clinic. They'll be wondering what's going on and Jo will be sinking without trace. I tell you what, I'll be ready for that take-away tonight. I don't know what happened to lunch.'

'You need to eat, Kate, you'll fade away,' he mimicked, and she threw the paper at him, stood up and walked out, a smile she tried to hide peeking out around the edges of her façade. He put the paper back on the table and followed her, whistling softly under his breath.

Life was suddenly looking a whole lot better…

It was funny how quickly something could become a habit.

He brought supper round to hers in the end that night because the children had settled without a murmur—a lovely Thai curry which he had delivered, much healthier than the

Indian cholesterol-fest she'd taken to his place, in deference to their livers, he said—and they ate it in the kitchen, with the communicating door open so they could listen. Then the following night, because there was a bit left in the bottle of wine he'd brought round, she took it back and they sat and watched the television for an hour and argued about a documentary and she went to bed with a smile on her face.

They weren't on call that weekend, blissfully, and she decided to give herself the luxury of a lie-in on Saturday morning.

She reckoned without the sound of James's children, though, all the little shrieks and squeals and the sound of running feet on the landing. And his deep, gruff voice shushing them, then the giggles because he must have caught them and picked them up, because the shrieks got louder and the running feet stopped.

She realised she was smiling. Nuts. She should be cross at losing her lie-in, but she found she wasn't. Far from it. It was lovely to hear the sound of happy children.

Especially James's happy children, after all they'd had to endure recently.

She got up, showered quickly and went downstairs in her scruffy old robe, her hair twisted up in a towel, and put the kettle on to boil while she got dressed. Then she heard a crash and a scream, and without even thinking about it she whipped the door open and ran through, to find James sitting at the bottom of the stairs with Rory on his lap, rubbing his knee and hugging him, while Freya hovered on the top step with her eyes like saucers.

'Freya, sweetheart, come here, he's all right,' she said softly, running up the stairs to her and scooping her up. She carried her back down and sat on the bottom step next to them with the toddler snuggled on her lap. 'Are you OK, Rory?'

'I fell downstairs,' he said, hiccuping, and James pulled his head in hard against his chest and rubbed it lovingly.

'You're all right, darling. It's OK. Let's just put some ice on it.'

'It's OK now,' he said. Wriggling off his father's lap, he got to his feet and limped through to the kitchen. 'Can I still have the last cake?' he asked, and James rolled his eyes and grinned at her.

'Is that what this is about? The last cake?' she asked, and he chuckled.

'Yeah. I thought he'd get dressed, but he just ran and opened the stairgate and slipped on his pyjamas. They always fall down, he's got such a skinny little bottom. He's OK.'

He'd said that so many times she wondered who he was trying to convince, but, following Rory into the kitchen, it seemed that he was probably right, because the boy was sitting at the table with his legs swinging, munching happily on a muffin and looking victorious.

'F'eya muffin!' Freya said, holding out her hand and opening and shutting it like a little starfish, but Rory wasn't giving up his muffin for anyone, and James was starting to look desperate, so she intervened.

'I tell you what, I've got some lovely chocolate biscuits next door,' she told them, and Rory stopped eating and Freya stopped crying and swivelled her head round and looked up at her hopefully. James just shrugged.

'Whatever,' he said, and she carried Freya through, Rory limping behind them, and they had tea and biscuits in her sitting room in front of cartoons, and it was just like having one of her brothers there with his kids.

Except for one very glaring difference. None of her brothers, whether blood, adoptive or foster, had ever made her feel the way James did. Good job, too, she thought, because her thoughts were seriously X-rated, but he just looked so good in those lovely washed-out old jeans with the top button undone and a T-shirt dragged on hastily and those somehow curiously sexy bare feet propped up on her coffee-table as if he belonged there.

'There's an icepack in my freezer if you think he needs it,' she told James, and he went and investigated and came back with it a moment later, wrapped in a tea-towel, and laid it over Rory's knee.

'I think it's fine,' he said, peering at it as he covered it, 'but it won't hurt to be careful. And as for you, young lady, I think you've had enough biscuits.'

'I think we all have, probably,' Kate said with a laugh, and offloading his daughter onto his lap, she put them back in the kitchen and came back, removing the towel as she did so and shaking out her hair. It tumbled over her shoulders like wet rope, and she sighed. 'I'll never get a comb through it,' she said, and looked up to find him watching her oddly.

Very oddly, as if he, too, was having X-rated thoughts, and the breath jammed in her throat.

Oh, help. If this wasn't one-sided, if they were going to become crazily aware of each other all the time, it was going to make working with him a nightmare.

She looked away hastily, scooped up their cups and turned off the television. 'Sorry, guys, I have to get dressed and sort my hair out. You'll have to go home.'

'What—properly home?' Rory said, looking aghast, and James, catching his expression, looked gutted.

'Next door, silly,' she said with a grin. 'Go on. Off you go. I won't be long.'

'Then can we come back?'

'Rory,' James said firmly, steering him towards the door with a hand on his shoulder and propelling him through it. 'Thanks for the tea and biscuits.'

'My pleasure,' she said, blowing a kiss to Freya, and he shut the door and left her in peace.

Except it didn't feel like peace, it felt curiously empty and lonely…

James heard the door open and saw Kate come out of her house. Opening his door, he hailed her.

'Kate! I need to speak to your parents.'

'Why?' she asked, turned back and coming towards him. 'Is there a problem?'

'No, not at all. I just need to sort out something about rent.'

'James, they won't take anything.'

'Then we'll move out.' He was adamant about it. 'They must have a tariff—some kind of letting fee.'

'No, they don't,' she said a little too quickly. 'It's only used for the family. We call it a holiday cottage, but it's really just a guest annexe. And you're my guest, so that's fine.'

Was she lying? Impossible to know, but there were all sorts of overheads. 'I need to pay the running costs, at least,' he protested. 'I need to speak to them, Kate. Today.'

'Well, come with me, then, I'm going over there now.'

So he rounded up the children from in front of the television and they all trailed across the farmyard and into the lovely old Tudor house that was her family home.

Sue was in the kitchen, up to her elbows in flour. 'Dan's coming for lunch tomorrow, so I thought I'd get ahead a bit,' she told Kate. 'He's got a new girlfriend.'

'Oh. Good. About time. Dan's one of my foster-brothers,' she explained to James. 'He's been a bit of a nightmare, but he's lovely now and things are really starting to work out for him.'

Andrew came in then, and before James could say a word, she greeted him with, 'Hi, Dad, James has some notion about paying the overheads on the barn—he seems to have some fixation about rent, but I explained that we don't rent it out. I told him you'd sort out the meter readings and things.'

'Of course. I'll see to it. Don't worry about it, James, it's all very straightforward.'

'Can't I just rent it from you?'

'Oh, no. That would cause havoc with the tax man. No, we'll just read the meter. That'll be the easiest thing.'

Her father didn't miss a beat, so if they were lying to him, they were doing it very proficiently, he thought, and gave up arguing. He'd buy them something as a thank-you when they were finally able to go home again. Whenever that might be…

'On the subject of the barn, Kate said something about the family using it over Christmas. Is that right? Because if it is, we can move back to our house for a while. We can always wash at my mother's, but I don't want to be in the way. It sounds like you'll have quite a crowd.'

'You won't be in the way, and of course you won't take the children back to that cold place over Christmas and unsettle them even more,' Sue said adamantly. 'In fact, what are you doing for Christmas?' she asked, and he realised he hadn't even considered it.

'No plans,' he said. 'My mother's spending it with her sister. My aunt was recently widowed and she hasn't been well. That's been arranged for ages. As for me and the kids, well, we haven't really thought about it, have we, kids?'

'I've thought about it,' Rory said, running his finger

through the dusting of flour on the kitchen table that Sue was
rolling the pastry out in. 'I want a big tree, and a stocking,
and I'm going to write a letter to Father Christmas. Kate, will
you help me write it?'

'What about me?' he asked, but Rory shook his head.

'I want Kate to help me,' he said stubbornly.

James couldn't argue any more. It might never happen, but
anyway he had better things to worry about, because Freya
had seen a dog come in and was trying to wriggle out of his
arms.

'Doggy!' she was saying insistently, and he looked down
a little uncertainly at the black Labrador sniffing at her toes.

'Is it OK with children?' he asked, and Sue chuckled.

'If you don't mind them being washed. Mungo's a sweetie.
She'll be fine with him.'

She was more than fine. She was in love. She stroked and
patted and giggled, and he wagged and slurped until she was
washed from end to end, and they ended up curled up together
in a heap on an old blanket beside the Aga while she pulled
his ears gently.

'Children need germs,' Andrew said, reading his mind, and
James just laughed and let them get on with it. Frankly, to see
them both so happy, Rory helping Sue put dollops of mince-
meat into the little pies while Freya stroked Mungo's ears and
crooned to him, was such a relief after the last year and a half
that he didn't care if they caught something dreadful.

It would almost be worth it just for this one morning.

'There, all done. Now I'm going to put them in the oven and
clear up. Kate, if you're not doing anything, why don't you
and James and the children take the dogs for a walk down by
the river? There might be some ducks.'

'Can we feed them?' Rory asked excitedly, running over to Kate and looking hopefully up into her eyes.

As if she could resist that, even if she'd wanted to. She smiled at him and got up. 'Sure. Mum, got any bread?'

'In the breadbin—there's a bit of corn bread that's past its sell-by date. James, have you got boots?'

'Ah. No.'

'That's fine,' Kate said. 'We have boots here in every conceivable size from tiny tots up to something huge. What size are your feet?'

'Ten.'

'Easy. Come on, then, lazybones, up you get,' she said to him. 'Freya? Coming to feed the ducks with Mungo?'

'Doggy coming?' she asked, and Kate nodded. 'He's coming. So's Badger.'

'Have you got a badger?' Rory asked, and she thought if his eyes got any bigger they'd fall out of his head.

'No. Just a dog called Badger. We've got badgers on the farm, though—and foxes and rabbits and squirrels and pheasants and—oh, all sorts.'

'Good grief,' James said faintly. 'It sounds like a wildlife park.'

'It is a bit. Then there are the farm animals. I'll show you those, if you like, kids. They belong to my uncle. He's got sheep and goats and cows.'

'*Wow!*'

She was wrong about the eyes. They could get bigger without falling out.

'Right, boots. James, try these. Rory, what size are your feet?'

It took a few minutes to sort them all out, then they needed thick coats and scarves and gloves, and then they were ready, the dogs bouncing and wagging their tails at the door. She took them down the lane to the ford so the kids could splash in the river, and they shrieked and giggled and everything was going fine until Freya fell over and got her mittens muddy.

Then James scooped her up, cleaned her off and sat her on his shoulders, and they walked back up round behind the farm to see the animals, and Rory climbed on a gate and scratched a goat's ears and Kate thought she'd never seen such a transformation from the children she'd first met.

'They seem to be having fun,' she said to James when he put Freya down and let her feed the ducks on the pond.

'They are. There hasn't been enough of that in the last few months. We had a good time in the summer, but that seems ages ago, and since Rory started school and I've been trying to find a job and a childminder, it's all been a bit more fraught. And as for the boiler…'

He rolled his eyes, and she smiled ruefully. 'I had a car like your life once. Every time I started it, something else fell off or went wrong.' She felt her smile fade. 'Still, at least I could sell the car.' Unlike his life, or her marriage.

He gave her a wry grin. 'Hey, it's not all bad. We're getting there—particularly, this week, thanks to you. I don't know what we would have done without the barn.'

'You would have found a way. Tom and Fliss have got a flat. They could have put you up. There are lots of options.'

'I'm more than happy with this one,' he said softly, and she followed his gaze to the children who were standing on the path by the pond, the dogs lined up in front of them sitting at attention, eyes fixed hopefully on their hands while they fed the ducks and the dogs in turn. And then he shifted his gaze to her, those strangely piercing blue eyes staring right down into her soul.

'More than happy. I owe you, Kate. Big time.'

She tried to smile, but her lips wouldn't really co-operate, and her lungs had forgotten how to work. 'I'll bear it in mind—I'm sure there'll come a time when I need a favour.'

'Make sure you ask me.'

'I will.'

It was one of those odd, timeless moments when the world seems to come to a halt. Their eyes locked, and she could feel herself swaying towards him, drawn in by his warmth and sincerity and downright sex appeal, and then suddenly there was a shriek and a splash and the children were laughing, and as if the spell had been broken he stepped back, dragged his eyes away from hers and turned towards them, and the mood was gone.

Thank goodness. The last thing she needed was to get sucked in by him and his children. No matter how much she adored them.

Any of them.

Oh, no, no, no! Stop it!

She called the dogs, and James gathered up the children and the bread bag and they headed back to the house.

'Perfect timing,' her mother said as they went back into a kitchen that smelt comforting and homely. 'I've made a big pot of Saturday soup, and the bread's cooling on the rack. Wash your hands, all of you, and come and sit down.'

That was it?

She didn't even bother to ask if they had plans, just laid the table and settled them all down like a mother hen with her chicks under her wings while Andrew carved up the loaf, and James felt the lump in his throat growing ever bigger.

'I don't like soup,' Rory told Kate doubtfully, but she just laughed and leant over, her dark head next to his.

'You'll like my mother's Saturday soup. It's got bacon and beans and all sorts of stuff. Everybody likes Saturday soup,' she told him confidently, and, sure enough, he did. Not only liked it, he went back for more.

Twice.

So did James, and even Freya had a respectable helping. Then Sue put an apple pie down in the middle of the table, and a steaming jug of custard, and it just got better.

'So what are you wearing for the wedding party tonight?' Sue asked Kate as she passed her a bowl, and for a second James thought she was going to drop it. And the look in her eyes was—

'Oh, damn. I'd forgotten. Is it really tonight?'

'Yes—oh, Kate, you can't have forgotten! You bought the present weeks ago.'

'I know. Um—the red dress, I suppose? It's sort of Christmassy and dressy enough. Fiddle. I'd really forgotten about it.'

Her mother gave her a keen look. 'Will you be all right?' she asked softly, and Kate lifted her shoulders a fraction.

'I suppose so. I'll have to be, won't I? I just—'

'Hate going alone?'

Her smile was wry. 'Absolutely.' And then she turned to James and said, 'My brother's brother-in-law is getting married to my ex's sister. And he'll be there.'

'Ouch.'

'What's an ex?'

'A has-been,' she said to Rory without looking at him.

'What's a has-been?'

'Someone who was a friend a long time ago,' James said,

modifying the truth just a little and watching Kate out of the corner of his eye. 'Somebody who's not a friend any more.'

'Why? Did you do something wrong so he doesn't like you?'

'Rory, stop asking questions and eat your apple pie,' he said, watching Kate carefully, then, before he had time to think about it too much, he said very softly, 'Would it help if you weren't alone?'

Her eyes flew to his, and her lips parted in surprise, then soft colour warmed her cheeks and she looked away, pressing her lips together.

'You don't need to do that.'

'Would you like me to?'

'It's an imposition.'

'Kate, yes or no?'

She looked across at her mother. 'Are you free to babysit?'

Sue didn't hesitate. In fact, if anything she looked quite enthusiastic. 'Of course,' she said.

'Then—yes, please. If you really don't mind, I'd be very grateful.'

'Of course I don't mind.'

'It's black tie—is that a problem?'

He shook his head. 'No. No problem.' Or he didn't think it was. He just had to find his suit.

'And that'll make us quits.'

'Quits?'

'On the favour front.'

She must be mad if she thought that taking her out for the evening could in any way be counted as a favour, but he let it go. For now.

When he finally got the children away from the table, he took them back to the house and dug out a few more changes of clothes for them, then took out his DJ and dress shirt. Goodness knows if it needed a clean. He couldn't even remember the last time he'd worn it. Two years ago? The Christmas ball, when Rory had been two and a half and Beth hadn't even realised she was pregnant.

Ah, hell.

He chucked it in the car, remembered his black dress shoes at the last minute and went and found them, too, then loaded up the children, locked the house and headed back. She was there outside the barn, tidying up a tub of pansies by her front door, and as they drove in she straightened up, lifting her hair back out of her eyes and smiling at them all, and he felt a tug of something long forgotten and probably totally inappropriate deep in his gut.

'Got everything you need?'

'Even the shoes,' he said wryly. 'What time's kick-off?'

'Seven for seven-thirty. We need to leave about a quarter to. Is that all right?'

'Sure. Knock on the door when you're ready.'

He took the children inside, found an iron in the kitchen and pressed his shirt, checked his suit and cleaned his shoes. Thankfully, there was some universal shoe cream stashed under the sink. He bathed the children, gave them scrambled eggs on toast and sat them down in front of the television while he showered.

Then at six-thirty, after he'd tucked the children up in bed and read them a story, he put the suit on. It was a lot looser on him, to his surprise, and he had to tighten the tabs on the waistband of the trousers, but he decided on balance it fitted better. He checked the pockets and found a handkerchief and a pair of tickets. Tickets for the hospital Christmas ball, his last Christmas with Beth.

He sat down on the edge of the bed and stared at the tickets for a moment. He could remember the event, but he could hardly remember Beth. What had she been wearing? Black, probably. She always wore black. He couldn't remember.

With a sigh he stood up and dropped the tickets into the waste-paper basket, and before he had time to think about it any more, he slipped off his wedding ring and put it in the bedside table drawer.

It was time to move on. Time to start living again, not only for him, but for Kate, too.

CHAPTER SIX

'Wow. Smart place.'

'Smart people,' she said flatly. 'I never really fitted.'

'So why are you here?'

Her laugh felt a little hollow. 'My brother's brother-in-law Adam is a lovely guy. And I got on really well with Jenny, my sister-in-law. And it's not really her fault her brother's a cold-hearted, self-centred bastard.'

'Ouch.'

'Oh, ignore me, I'm just bitter. But he's not a nice man. Pity I didn't work that out before I married him.'

'So why didn't you?'

She shrugged. 'I don't really know. He can be very charming, but he didn't want me to be a doctor, and I think he always imagined I'd give it all up to have his babies and settle down. He was a bit shocked when I refused, but I really wasn't ready. There were things I needed to do first.'

'I'm surprised,' he said quietly. 'I would have thought you'd have jumped at the chance of having children. You're wonderful with them, and they adore you. Well, mine do, anyway. They're wearing your name out talking about you.'

She gave a guilty little laugh. 'I'm sorry about that. They're lovely. I have to admit I adore them, too.'

'So how come you didn't want children when you were married?' he asked, and she shrugged.

'I did, in a way, but apart from the fact that I didn't think he'd make much of a father, like I said, I had things to do first.'

'And have you done them yet?'

'Some of them. Not all.' And not all of them mattered, of course. Some were just things to fill the future she could see stretching out ahead of her like a long, empty road.

'So what's his name?'

She dragged herself back to the present. 'Jon—short for Jonathan.'

'Right. Is there anything else I need to know about him?'

'Apart from the fact that the last time I saw him I was recovering from surgery? Not really.'

She didn't look at him, but she heard his indrawn breath, and after a moment he moved on.

'So—will there be anyone from work here?'

'Good grief, no,' she said, laughter bubbling up at the very thought. 'Two totally different worlds.'

'And ne'er the twain shall meet?'

She flashed him a smile. 'Something like that. Right, shall we?'

'I'm ready when you are.'

'I'm ready as I'll ever be.'

He was there by the time she'd worked out where the doorhandle was and picked the present up off the floor, and he extended her a firm, warm hand and helped her out, then closed the door and offered her his elbow.

'Such a gentleman,' she teased, and he smiled.

'I can be—when my boss isn't giving me strain.'

'I'll have to bear that in mind,' she said. Straightening her shoulders and pulling her wrap a little tighter, she dredged up her most brilliant smile.

'Before we go in,' he said, pausing on the steps, his hand over hers in the crook of his elbow, and she turned and looked up at him questioningly. 'You look beautiful tonight,' he said, his voice a little gruff, and she felt a warm glow sweep over her.

'Thank you, James,' she said, a tiny tremor in her voice, and she ran her eyes over him and smiled. 'I have to say you don't look so bad yourself.'

'It's amazing what you can do with a bar of soap and a well-cut suit.' He grinned and inclined his head towards the doors. 'Shall we?'

She was fabulous.

Taut as a bowstring, but composed, dignified and very, very close to him.

He was introduced to her brother Michael, very like her, with the same warm brown eyes, and his pretty pregnant wife, Louise, who was the sister of the groom. They were lovely people, and very interested in him, he could tell, although they tried to be discreet.

'Don't get excited, he's a colleague and he's only here as a smokescreen,' she told them drily, but they didn't look any less interested or at all convinced, and he wondered what he was giving away, or if it was that Kate absolutely never went out with a man? And if so, why? Because it would get in the way of her achieving all her goals?

Something about that didn't fit, because she'd admitted she wanted children.

Which was a thought worthy of considerably more attention later, he decided, and filed it.

They chatted for a few minutes, but they were in demand and so he and Kate moved on. She introduced him to the blissfully happy bride and groom, Jenny and Adam, and a couple of other people, and all the time he was aware of the curious glances that followed them around the room.

Maybe she really never did go out with a man—in which case, thank goodness there was nobody from the hospital there, or the gossipmongers would be having a field day.

There was a finger buffet served by a diligent army of waiters, but he wasn't interested in food, or the free-flowing champagne that was circulating. The only thing that held his attention was Kate, and he was riveted.

Especially when she introduced him to Jon.

The dreaded ex.

She was brilliant—and James loathed him on sight.

'Katherine—how nice to see you!' he said, hardly sparing James a glance. 'You're looking well.'

Better than she had when she was recovering from surgery? That was when Kate had said she'd last seen him, and James had to stifle the urge to knock the self-satisfied smile down his throat. He remembered the wicked scar around her ribs and his jaw clenched. Had this man been in any way responsible for that?

'Thank you, Jon.' Nobody else would have realised how false her sparkling smile was, but he knew the effort it must have cost her, and his hand settled on the hollow of her back in support, and he felt her lean back into him.

'It's lovely to see you, too,' she said brightly. 'You're looking well.' And then she added innocently, 'The extra weight suits you.'

He nearly choked at the man's expression, but managed to contain the laugh.

'Ever the wit,' Jon said a little crisply, his smile slipping a little, and then assessing eyes swivelled James's way. 'I hadn't realised you weren't alone tonight. Aren't you going to introduce me?'

'Of course. Jon, this is James McEwan. He's—'

'Good to put a face to a name,' James interrupted, cutting her off and taking charge of this one as he shook the man's hand. 'I've heard a lot about you. Kate and I are very…' He paused. '*Good* friends.' The emphasis wasn't lost, and Jon's eyebrows rose fractionally.

'Well, I hope she doesn't bore you to death,' he replied with a slightly mocking laugh. 'She's got a morbid obsession with cutting people up. Never could understand it. So what do you do?'

Oh, he was enjoying this. 'I cut people up,' he said deadpan.

'Oh, I might have known it, you're another bloody doctor,' Jon said with undisguised disgust, and then laughed again dismissively. 'Oh, well, Kate, you'll be all right with this one. He won't even notice when you work ludicrous hours.'

'Actually, he does notice, and he works even more ludicrous hours than I do, so, as you were kind enough to point out, we're well suited.'

And sliding an arm round his waist, she leant up against James and smiled like the cat that had got the cream.

'Pompous ass. I hope he never needs my attention,' James growled as Jon walked away to more interesting pastures, and she chuckled.

'Not a chance. He only goes private. That should have told me something. I still haven't worked out if I'm a lousy judge of character or if he's got worse as he's got older.'

'Both, probably. You're a bit inclined to see the good in people. Well, except me.'

'I see the good in you!' she protested, turning to face him, and his lips twitched.

'Not on my first day.'

'You were late because you'd been incompetent!'

He grinned. 'Fair cop. Fancy a dance?'

'Do you know, I think I do?'

She smiled at him, relaxing now the dreaded meeting was over, and he led her to the dance floor, just as the song finished and the music slowed, so he slid his arms round her and eased her up against him.

Oh, hell. Big mistake. Huge, massive mistake, because the feel of her body, soft and warm and very feminine against him, was enough to send him into meltdown.

He moved away a fraction, and the moment the beat speeded up he let her go and created a little space between them. Not too much. Just enough, so that he didn't have to feel her thighs brushing against his, her breasts pressing into his chest, her hands warm and light against his waist.

But he could still smell that intoxicating fragrance and in many ways it was worse because now he could watch her, and the sight of her body moving sinuously in time to the music was going to do his head in.

'I need a drink,' he said a trifle desperately, and led her away from the dance floor before he disgraced himself completely.

'Do you really need a drink? Or do you need to get out of here?'

'Can we? Before the bride and groom leave?'

'I'm sure we can. Knowing them, they'll be partying until three o'clock.' And then she added with a little grin, 'I've got a nice bottle of Merlot in my kitchen.'

Was he dreaming, or was that a very definite invitation in her eyes? He wasn't taking any chances.

'Give me a minute,' he said. Diving into the gents', he raided the conveniently full dispensing machine in the corner next to the hand-dryer. He could hardly get the coins into it his hands were shaking so badly. It was ridiculous. She probably didn't intend anything of the sort, but there was no way he was going back there unprepared.

Finally he managed the simple task, pulled open the drawer, slid the packet into his trouser pocket and turned round, just as Jon walked in.

'Ah, McEwan. Wondered where you were. Kate was looking lost. I think she suspects you've slipped off without her.'

'I doubt it,' he said drily. 'She knows I wouldn't do that. I keep my promises. You know—in sickness and in health, and all that…'

And without another word, he brushed past him and went out into the foyer.

'Did you see Jon?'

'I did. He said you were looking lost.'

'Liar. I was saying goodbye to my brother. Are you all set?'

'Yes. Let's go before we run into him again and I feel obliged to feed him his teeth.'

She gave a surprised little chuckle, and the sound of it warmed him to the soles of his shoes.

'Mum? We're back.'

'Oh, hello, darling, you're early,' her mother said, turning off the television and getting to her feet. 'Hello, James. So did you both have a good time?'

Kate just laughed. 'Hardly. Well, the party was fine, but Jon was as obnoxious as usual.'

'I think you got your own back,' James replied, and her

mother raised a questioning eyebrow. 'She told him the extra weight suited him.'

Her mother's eyes widened and filled with laughter. 'Oh, Kate, you are naughty.'

'I know. It was great. He had the nerve to tell me I was looking better!'

'Oh, stupid man. Still, you got through it.'

'She more than got through it, she was fabulous, and we did have a good time,' James said beside her, and her mother looked from him to Kate and back again, and a tiny, knowing smile flickered around the corners of her mouth.

'Good. Well, I'm glad you enjoyed it. I haven't heard a sound out of the children, by the way. They must have worn themselves out this morning on your walk.'

'Probably. Thank you so much for looking after them.'

'Any time. It's good to see Kate getting out. She should do it more.'

Just go, Mum, she thought, wondering what she was going to say next, but she just kissed her on the cheek and went out. 'Don't forget Dan's coming for lunch tomorrow. You're all invited, if you'd like to come. It's open house.'

'It's always open house,' she said ruefully as her mother closed the door. 'I've never known it be anything else. It's a wonder she doesn't drag the postman in and give him breakfast.'

'She's wonderful,' James said, and she smiled.

'I know, and I love her to bits. She's a brilliant mother. Right, I'm going to get out of this dress.'

'That's a shame. You look lovely in it.'

She hesitated. It itched, and the bra was too tight over her ribs, but the look in his eyes…

'OK, then. Just give me a minute.'

And she went through into her half of the barn, ran upstairs and wriggled out of the hard, uncomfortable strapless bra that pressed on her ribs, and went back down, hoping that the boning in the dress was adequate and that she wouldn't fall out of it and embarrass herself to bits.

He was standing in her kitchen. He'd shed the jacket and left the bow-tie dangling when he'd undone the first three buttons of his shirt, so she could just see a tantalising glimpse of his broad, muscular chest, and he looked amazing.

Warm and relaxed and just so damn sexy she was going to make a fool of herself.

'Is this the wine you were talking about?'

'Do you see another one?'

He grinned. 'I didn't know if you had a secret stash.'

'No secret stash. I know I seem to have done nothing else since you moved in, but I don't really drink. Occasionally I like a glass after a particularly long day, so I keep a bottle in stock. You've obviously just caught me in a weak moment.' Why was she justifying herself? 'Here, you can earn your keep and open it.'

She passed him two wineglasses and rummaged in a cupboard for crisps.

'Sour cream and spring onion or sea salt and cracked pepper?' she asked, waggling the packets at him.

'Whatever. You choose.'

'Well, I like both, that's why I bought them.'

'Sea salt.'

'Right.'

They headed through to the sitting room, and she put on some soft bluesy music, turned the lights down low and sat beside him on her sofa, the crisps between them and their feet propped side by side on the coffee-table.

'Tell me about Dan,' he said, munching the crisps, and she rolled her head towards him and smiled.

'Dan's lovely. He's been a bit of a wild child—he's mixed race, and his father didn't want to know and his teenage mother's family were horrified to have a coloured child thrust into their white middle-England midst and kicked them out, so he didn't really belong, and he went off the rails a bit—stealing cars, joy-riding, that sort of thing. Mum and Dad sorted him out, though, and he's been to uni and he's a motoring journalist now. He's doing well, but his self-esteem is still a bit shaky and so he doesn't expect his relationships to work. He's always surprised when people like him.'

James frowned. 'That's tough. I really would have thought in this day and age it wouldn't make any difference what your ethnic background was.'

'And you think I'm naïve?' she teased, and pushed the crisps towards him. 'Come on, eat up or I'm going to have to finish them and then I'll be like a house.'

'Yeah, right. I can see that happening.' He shifted a little so he was facing her, and she could feel his eyes on her like lasers. She felt instantly self-conscious, and had to stop herself forcibly from tugging at the top of her dress.

'Don't.'

'What?'

'Look at me like that.'

'Like what?' He sounded surprised.

'Like—I don't know. Like you're studying an insect.'

He laughed. 'Actually, I was just looking at you. I find it's easier to talk to people when I can see them. And, anyway, I like looking at you. You're beautiful.'

She felt herself colour. That was the second time he'd said it tonight, and it made her feel vaguely uncomfortable.

'Hardly,' she replied. 'I mean, I know the dress is lovely, but it's just me.' She shrugged, and he just shook his head slowly.

'What's wrong? Why can't you take a compliment, Kate?'

She forced herself to meet his eyes. 'I can—when it isn't a blatant lie.'

'It's not a lie.'

'James, I'm not beautiful. I may be reasonably attractive, but—'

'Kate, you're beautiful. Believe me.'

Could she? He sounded sincere enough, but he hadn't seen—

'Do you know why I was in hospital?' she said abruptly.

'No, but I'm guessing it was something to do with the scar on your ribs?'

She sucked in her breath and met his eyes, shocked. 'How do you know?'

He looked a little awkward. 'The changing-room door was open. I glanced up. I wasn't spying, I just…saw you.'

'Oh, God.' She closed her eyes and turned her head away, colour flooding her cheeks. She felt a flicker of guilt, because she'd sneaked another peek at him, but it had never occurred to her that he'd do the same. 'I didn't realize…'

'Tell me about it,' he prompted gently. 'What happened? Was it something to do with Jon?'

'Jon? Good grief, no. He's a pompous ass but he's not violent. No, a patient lashed out at me and kicked me in the ribs. One of them punctured my lung and nicked the pulmonary vein. It was pretty exciting for a while, I gather.'

'For heaven's sake! How hard did he kick you?'

'Hard. He had steel toecaps on. I was called down to A and E to examine him because he'd got a query appendix. I poked him, and he didn't like it—especially when I told him there was nothing wrong with him.'

'Idiot.'

'Oh, absolutely. I should have been more careful.'

'Not you! Him!'

'Oh.' Funny, she'd got so used to thinking it was her fault—and was that Jon's fault?—that she'd lost sight of the simple truth. 'Yes, I suppose he was an idiot. But it scared me. And I hate the dark now.'

'What's the dark got to do with it?'

'Well, that's where it happened—in the car park. He followed me when I left work.'

'You weren't still examining him?'

'No, there was nothing wrong with him so I'd got rid of him ages before. He was just trying to skive off work, and I made him look a fool. So he hung around waiting for me and left me lying on the ground in the car park. Luckily someone came along shortly afterwards, otherwise I would have died. And all Jon could say was that it was my own fault, he'd told me I worked stupid hours and if I'd been at home where I belonged it wouldn't have happened. He'd had to cancel an important dinner and it had cost him thousands in lost contracts.'

'All this, while you were lying in bed in hospital?'

She nodded. 'I told him to go away—told him if his stupid contracts were more important than me then I didn't want to see him again. He took all my things round to my parents' and left them there on the porch, and that was it. Finish. The end of my marriage.'

'You're better off without him.'

'Oh, tell me about it. It's not all bad, though. He's paid for this.' She waved a hand at the room and dredged up a smile. 'The conversion work, anyway. Both sides. I had it done for the family, as a thank you, and at the moment I'm living here. I've got another house, but...'

'But?'

She sighed. 'I just don't like going back there in the dark, so I rent it out. And I've been fine here, mostly, but—well, Pete Graham brought it all back a bit.'

'I'm sure. You should have said something. I would have made sure you didn't have to deal with him.'

'James, it's not a problem, I can handle it.'

'Of course you can, but if you don't have to, why should you? And, anyway, what's all this got to do with whether or not you can take a compliment?'

She looked away. 'Well—you've seen the scar. It doesn't exactly enhance me.'

'I disagree,' he said softly. 'It adds another layer to the complex person I'm getting to know—and it certainly doesn't detract from you.'

'Doesn't it?'

'Of course not. Why should it? Has it put anybody else off?'

She couldn't look at him. 'I wouldn't know. I haven't been in a situation where the subject might arise.'

He stared at her. 'What? But—that's not a recent scar.'

'Three years old—nearly four.'

'And…' He frowned, then shook his head. 'You're unreal.'

The music came to an end, and he stood up and went and rummaged through her CDs. 'Choose what you like,' she told him, wondering what he'd go for, and to her surprise he put on an album of love songs that she'd bought in a lonely moment, and came back to her and held out his hand, his eyes unreadable in the soft lighting.

'Dance with me,' he murmured.

Her heart lurched. 'Really? Here?'

'Why not?' he asked softly. 'It's better here. Nobody can see us.'

Because it was crazy, and silly, and so, so dangerous. If she touched him, she'd be lost. But she'd been dying to dance with him again, and he was just there, looking so damn sexy she couldn't resist him. And he didn't care about her scar...

She took his hand, let him pull her to her feet and moved into his arms, resting her head on his shoulder and feeling the fine, soft cotton of his shirt under her cheek. Her nose was close to his throat, and she could smell the clean citrus tang of his aftershave and the undercurrent of his own personal scent, warm and intoxicating. She rested her hands against his sides, her fingers splayed against his ribs, and she felt his breath ease out, teasing her hair, warm against her ear.

'You smell wonderful,' he murmured, nuzzling her cheek, his voice low and gruff and incredibly sexy.

She felt the brush of his thighs, the shift of his ribcage under her fingers, the heat of his hands against her waist, and then they slid down, cupping her bottom and easing her closer, and she felt heat pool low down in her body at the intimate contact.

'Kate?'

She lifted her head a fraction and his jaw grazed her forehead, the stubble just rough enough to excite. The touch of his lips was warm and gentle, coaxing as they glided over her skin, down her nose, across her cheek, then back again, drifting over her mouth, backwards and forwards, until finally they settled.

Her lips parted, and with a muffled sigh he lifted his hands and tunnelled his fingers through her hair, holding her steady as he deepened the kiss and took her mouth with a hunger that both terrified and excited her.

She'd *never* been kissed like this, as if he'd die without her, and it was shocking and wonderful and incredibly potent. She lifted a hand to his jaw, loving the feel of it, smooth and yet rough against her palm, driving her higher. She needed more than this, needed to kiss him back, needed…

Sliding her hand around the back of his neck, she pulled him down harder against her, opening her mouth to the full onslaught of his.

It was like putting a match to tinder. One of his hands slid down, cupping her bottom and lifting her hard against him, and she gasped at the shockingly intimate contact of her body with his. She could feel his response, knew what it was doing to him, what it was doing to her, also, and her resistance crumbled.

What resistance? She didn't *want* to resist. She wanted James—here, now, no questions asked. She needed him.

She'd die without him.

He drew away, lifting his head a fraction and resting his forehead against hers while his chest rose and fell against hers and his breath was hot against her face.

'Kate, this is getting out of hand,' he said raggedly.

'Yes.'

'You'd better stop me now.'

'No.'

He groaned softly, then lifted his head a little more and stared down into her eyes. 'Are you sure? We can't undo this later.'

'Do you want to?'

'No. Hell, no. I want to take you upstairs to your room and make love to every single square inch of you.'

Delicious promise shivered over her, leaving her strung tight with anticipation, and she stared up into his eyes, his pupils black, rimmed with blue fire. His lips were parted, his face taut, and she could feel his self-control making his body tremble under her hands.

She slid her hand down his arm, threaded her fingers through his and led him up the stairs to her room.

She didn't turn on the light, but the moon was full and the light poured through the roof window and streamed across the bed, silvering everything it touched.

She turned to him, freeing the buttons of his shirt one by one, taking out the cufflinks and throwing them aside, then running her hands slowly over his chest, his shoulders, his arms, back down to the bottom of his ribcage, turning her hands over so her knuckles grazed his skin and made him suck in his breath.

'Kate…'

'Shh.'

Suddenly brave, her eyes locked with his and she let her fingers explore him, finding the catch on his trousers and freeing it, sliding the zip down slowly, so slowly, while he held his breath and stared back at her with those mesmerising, fiery eyes.

The backs of her fingers brushed the thick, solid ridge of his erection, and he exhaled sharply and took her hands and lifted them away.

'Enough,' he grated. 'Please. I need to see you.'

His arms went round her, his fingers searching while she waited impatiently, unable to think about anything except being close to him. 'How the hell do I get into this?' he growled, and she remembered.

'Side,' she said, lifting her arm, and he found the tab and unzipped it, then grasping the fabric, he tugged her dress down. For a moment it resisted, then slid away and puddled at her feet, and he sucked in his breath, his eyes fixed on her.

Oh, Lord. Her scar. She'd forgotten…

He reached out a hand and touched not the scar but one

breast, his thumb skimming lightly over the tip, making the air lodge in her throat.

'James…'

'I want you so much,' he muttered unevenly.

His head bent, and she felt the warmth of his breath on her skin just moments before his tongue brushed her nipple, circling it, teasing it as his thumb had done. Then he drew it into his mouth and suckled it, while his other hand cupped and kneaded the other one, rolling her nipple between finger and thumb until she thought the sensation would push her right over the edge.

Her legs buckled, and he caught her and lifted her, putting her down in the middle of the bed and carrying right on exploring her with his mouth. His lips moved on, over her ribs, feathering a gentle, healing kiss along the scar before moving down, his breath hot across her abdomen. His fingers traced the edge of the audacious red French knickers she'd been wearing under the dress.

'You wicked woman,' he murmured, running his finger round the loose leg, grazing her most sensitive spot with the back of his knuckle, making her gasp. 'Oh, yes,' he whispered. Bending his head, he laid his mouth over the aching mound and blew hot breath on her, so that she cried out, bucking under his hands.

'James, please…'

'I thought you'd never ask,' he teased, but his voice was tight with control, and as he shucked off his trousers and reached for the pocket, she felt her heart nearly stop.

Oh, it had been so long. What if she disappointed him? What if—

His hand slid over her, curling around her breast, down over her ribs, across the flat plane of her abdomen, then on, catching the lacy knickers and peeling them away as he ran his hand slowly, firmly down her legs and over her feet, then drew his hand back up, his fingertips skimming the spot behind her knee that seemed to link with every erogenous zone she had and set them all on fire.

Then he parted her legs, kneeling between them and staring down at her, his breath coming hard and fast. She couldn't see his eyes, but she could feel the burning intensity of them as he lowered himself down and touched her, his hand testing her, parting her, making way for the long, slow thrust of his body entering hers.

'Kate…'

Her name was a breath on his lips, and she wrapped herself around him and drew him in, her heart opening to him as surely as her body, and then he started to move, slowly at first, then faster, harder, carrying her along until she felt the first tightening of her orgasm claiming her.

'James!' she sobbed, and then he was with her, driving her over the edge, his body shuddering against her in release, until at last he rolled to his side, drawing her with him. Pressing his lips to hers, he cradled her close against his chest until their breathing slowed and their hearts settled and the silence of the night enfolded them…

CHAPTER SEVEN

HE DUCKED out of lunch with Dan and his girlfriend, taking the children over to the house instead to check that everything was all right, and then doing some work in the garden.

It was a lovely day, and he felt full of energy and life and hope.

Not that he thought anything would come of his relationship with Kate. She'd made it clear that she wasn't ready yet to settle down and have a family, and the one thing he could be sure of was that he had a family!

But their love-making had been spectacular, and he wasn't sure he could sit at her parents' table and have a civilised conversation with the frantic, desperate sounds she'd made last night still echoing in his ears. So he dressed the children up warmly, and they ran about in the garden and dug in the sandpit and Freya went on the swing and Rory pushed her, and he cleared the dead leaves and stems from the perennials and cut back some of the shrubs and started a bonfire, and then they went and bought burgers and shoestring fries for lunch and watched the fire burn down.

Then, when the sun started to get low in the sky, he took them back to Kate's. There was a sports car on the drive when they pulled in, and Andrew was at the woodpile with a huge log basket. He straightened up and waved as they got out of the car.

'James! We missed you at lunch. Have you had a good time?'

'Wonderful, thank you. We've been in the garden.'

'Well, come on in, we're in the drawing room—Sue's just made a pot of tea and there's cake and all sorts, not that anybody'll be able to eat another thing, but you know how she is. Come and join us and warm up.'

He glanced down at their clothes and shook his head ruefully.

'We're not really dressed for it, Andrew.'

'Nonsense! You're fine. Come on in. Dan's girlfriend's got a little boy just Rory's age. They'll have fun together.'

It was impossible to refuse without sounding rude, but he at least had to stall.

'I need to change Freya's nappy, and we really are grubby. Can you give us five minutes?'

'Of course. Take as long as you like, and let yourselves in—just follow the noise.'

He looked gorgeous—windswept and ruddy and full of the outdoors, and it suited him.

Kate smiled at him as he came in, and patted the sofa beside her, and after he'd greeted everyone and been introduced to Dan and Rachel and her little boy Sean, he sat down beside her with a muffled groan.

'Hi, there.'

'Hello again. Are you all right? I gather you've been gardening.'

'I have—and I haven't done it for years, so just about everything hurts!'

She chuckled. 'But you had a good day?'

'Great. We've cleared up a lot of the garden, and we had a fire.'

'I know, I can smell the woodsmoke on you, and you've got some colour in your cheeks, all of you. It sounds like you've had fun,' she said wistfully.

'We have. I'll probably regret it for a few days, but we had a good time.'

She hesitated. 'I don't like to spoil it, but I had a phone call from the hospital.'

He frowned and went still. 'About?'

'Tracy Farthing—her boyfriend was so grossed out by the idea of the hairball that he dumped her, so she tried to hang herself in the bathroom from her IV line.'

He dropped his head back and closed his eyes. 'Oh, my God. Poor little kid. Are Psych on it?'

'Oh, yes, but she's very distressed.'

'I'm sure she is, and it won't help her at all.'

'No, it won't,' she agreed. 'What an idiot.'

'Her or the boyfriend?'

'Both, but I meant him. What is wrong with people that they have to hurt each other all the time?'

'He probably just needs some counselling himself. I think it was quite a serious relationship. I had a chat with her. You know they were sleeping together?'

'That doesn't necessarily mean it's serious,' she said. Why should it? James had slept with her last night, but she was under no illusions about the long-term nature of their relationship. After all, he'd run a mile that morning rather than have lunch with her family.

'I think she was serious,' he said thoughtfully. 'Maybe more than him, I don't know. Kids are complicated, and hormones are dreadful things.'

'Not always,' she murmured, and she saw his eyes flare.

'No, not always,' he agreed with a lazy smile. Turning his attention back to the children, he drank his tea and made polite conversation with her family while all she could think about was getting him away from them, settling the children for the night and taking him back to bed.

He went and saw Tracy on Monday morning, and found her subdued and miserable.

'Hiya,' he said, and perched on the edge of her bed. 'You've had a bit of an eventful weekend, I hear. I'm sorry about your boyfriend.'

She turned her head away. 'He said I'm disgusting.'

'You're not disgusting, Tracy. You didn't even know you were doing it and, anyway, it's not so much disgusting as worrying, because it can make you ill. Do you think it would help if I talked to him?'

'The shrink was going to do that, but he wouldn't see him. Anyway, it's over. I'm dumped, and that's that.'

Her voice broke, and she started to cry, but then pulled herself together and sat up carefully. 'I'm all right, Mr McEwan. I'll be OK. I'm not going to try anything silly like that again.'

He wasn't in the least bit sure she was OK, but he left her, promising to have a word with her boyfriend if he wanted to talk about it, and he went back down to the main surgical unit to catch up with Kate.

'So how is she?' she asked.

He shrugged. 'Pretty down. I said I'd try to have a word with the boyfriend if he comes in—maybe ring him if he doesn't. I might be able to get through to him.'

'When the others haven't?' she asked, looking doubtful.

'Well, it's worth a try. The whole mental health team seems to be female, so are most of the ward staff—I just thought maybe, being a man, he might be more likely to listen to me and I might be able to bring a different perspective to it.'

'Well, as you say, it's worth a try.'

'If he even agrees to speak to me, which is a bit of a shot in the dark. So, how is it down here? Anything I should know about?'

'Pete Graham—he's looking good. I was hoping we could discharge him now the brother's out of the way. His mother said he can go home and she'll look after him. He lives in a bedsit or something, so as long as he does go home to her, that's fine with me. Do you agree?'

He felt his eyebrow climb. 'You're asking my opinion?'

She smiled wryly. 'Only for a male perspective, since we're on the subject. So—do you think he's ready?'

'I think he's ready to be discharged, but only if the brother really is out of the way. We don't want him getting bail and going back for another go.'

'No, we don't, but we can't babysit the man, he's twenty-four and it's up to the police to make sure he's safe, not us. If you think he's fit, then he goes. We need the bed.'

'We always need the beds,' he pointed out, and wondered if she really thought Peter was ready or just wanted him out of the way, because of the uncomfortable reminders. No. He was ready. And they couldn't babysit him, she was right. 'OK, let's send him home and clear the bed. Did they have a busy weekend?'

'Looks like it. Let's hope tonight isn't busy, because we're on. Will your mother be able to look after the children?'

He shrugged. 'I don't know. I haven't spoken to her for a

day or two. To be honest I'm so frustrated with her I don't know what to think. Is it all right if she stays at the barn? Assuming I can get her to do it.'

'Of course it is! Don't be silly. Ring her and sort it out, James, and if she can't do it, bribe your childminder, because if we're busy, I'm going to need you.'

He gave her a keen look, then nodded and walked away, and she sighed. She couldn't stop being his boss just because they were sleeping together.

Or had done for two nights.

Not even slept, because of the children. Each time he'd gone back to his room afterwards and stayed there in case they woke, and she'd missed him.

Stupid. Stupid, stupid woman. Fancy letting him get so deeply under her skin so quickly. It didn't help that he was so damned good at it. No other man had ever made her feel the way he did, as if she'd die if he didn't touch her, and it wasn't even just that. There were the kids, as well, and she could so easily imagine them all together.

She picked up a pile of notes, glanced through them and made her way to her office. She'd catch up on some paperwork before her clinic started. If she didn't do it now, she'd never get it done.

And it would take her mind off James and his all too enchanting family.

'Mum, of course I'm speaking to you.'

'But only because you need me.'

He sighed. 'That's rubbish and you know it. We went into this knowing it was going to be hard, and you agreed to be there for them when I'm on call. If I'd known you were going to…' He broke off, and mentally changed 'be' to 'find it'. 'Find it so difficult, I would have made other arrangements in advance, or not taken the job. It's only for four months. Please, don't let me down.'

'It's not a case of letting you down.'

'Well, what the hell would you call it?' he said, hanging on to his temper with difficulty. 'If you really don't want to help us, then I'll see what I can set up for the New Year, but until then, I don't really see what else I can do. Kate's giving me grief as it is, and I don't want to annoy her any more than I have to. But I need to do this, and you need to help me, and accept that it won't be easy, that I'm a lone parent and there will be compromises. It can't be helped.'

'James, I find it so hard,' she said, sounding even more distressed. 'If only you hadn't let Beth die—if you'd made her have the treatment—'

He sighed shortly and rammed his hand through his hair. 'I didn't let Beth die, Mum, you know that. You know how much I loved her. It just happened. I had no say in it.'

'You could have made her get rid of Freya.'

'No. No, I couldn't have made her get rid of Freya, and I wouldn't have done. Anyway, it was too late, you know that. If she'd wanted a termination, I would have supported her, but she didn't. And it wasn't easy for any of us, and it won't be, ever, but it's the way it is and we have to move on. And I'm moving on. We've got a new house, I'm getting back to work, I'm making a new life for us all. And we need your help. Please. I can't do this without you, and you promised. God knows, I haven't asked you for much.'

His mother was silent for a moment, then she sighed. 'All right. I'll do it for now, but I'm really very uncomfortable about it, James. Freya's so unhappy.'

'No. She's not unhappy. She's fine. She's just a bit clingy, and she's getting better every day. Just see it through, Mum, please. Don't make it any harder. I'll pick them up from the childminder tonight and come round to you, then take you back to the barn and show you where everything is. If you could be ready at six, that would be good. I'll see you later.'

He hung up, let his breath out on a growl of frustration and slouched back in the chair.

'That sounded like a prelude to World War Three,' Kate said from behind him, and he spun the chair round and stared at her in horror, scrolling back through the conversation and groaning mentally.

'How long have you been there?'

'Long enough. She's giving you a hard time.'

'Yeah. She is, and there's nothing I can do about it. She's got this bee in her bonnet about me not being able to look after them, and every time she gets like this, it makes it true. So you're right. My child care is precarious.'

'Perhaps you need a nanny,' she suggested, settling on the edge of the desk, too close for his peace of mind. He made himself concentrate.

'No. Too much power. It was a disaster before—and, anyway, our house isn't fit for a nanny to live in. I can see me interviewing them in it. They'd run a mile.'

She laughed. 'It's not for long, and it's going to be lovely. Any idea when the plumber can do your boiler?'

'And the rest,' he said morosely. 'It should be finished some time in January, hopefully. Why? Is there a problem with the barn?'

'No, not at all. I was going to suggest that you move into my side for Christmas, and the gang can have your side, unless you think the children would be very disrupted by that, in which case I can come to you and we'll all share, but it will be a bit of a squash.'

'I can take them home…'

'Don't be silly, you'll freeze. Anyway, you're with us for Christmas so you may as well be staying there.'

'Are we?' He knew Sue had said something about it, but he wasn't aware of having accepted. 'Is your mother expecting us?'

'I thought so, and if your mother's elsewhere and you've got nothing better planned, you may as well join us. You're all more than welcome, and the kids'll love it, James. There'll be so many little ones for them to play with, and they'll all adore Freya. She'll be the baby of the family and she'll be spoiled to death.'

The baby of the family? Was that how she saw them? As part of the family?

He felt a longing so great it was almost a pain, and the idea of spending another lonely Christmas was just too much to contemplate.

'If you're sure.'

'Of course I'm sure. Mum would skin me if you didn't join us. And now, if you've finished with my desk, I've got letters to write. In fact, you could do some of them, they're your patients.'

And she handed him a sheaf of notes, shooed him out of her chair and settled down to dictate into a little hand-held recorder.

'Have you got another one of those?'

She opened the drawer, pulled out a second one and lobbed it at him. He caught it one-handed, tested it and, dropping into the chair on the other side of the desk, he flicked open the notes, refreshed his memory and started to dictate.

A few minutes later he realised she'd stopped talking and was watching him thoughtfully.

'What?'

'There's a job coming up.'

He frowned. 'Really?'

'Really. They're looking for a new consultant general surgeon, and they've asked me what I think about you.'

He put the recorder down slowly. 'And?'

She met his eyes frankly. 'I told them I had reservations about your child-care arrangements, but that in principle I thought you'd be an excellent choice.'

He sighed and ran a hand over his face. And she'd had to come in and hear him rowing with his mother over that very subject. Damn.

'What? Did you expect me to lie to them, James, just because we're sleeping together?'

He dropped his hand and stared at her. 'No. Not at all. I'd rather you didn't. It's only the truth. In fact, if us having a relationship outside work is going to make things awkward for you, then perhaps I should find alternative accommodation and we'll cool it off. I don't want you feeling compromised.'

Her eyes widened slightly, then she looked away. 'It's entirely up to you what you do about your accommodation, but you're more than welcome to stay. I've told you that over and over again.'

'And the rest?' he asked softly.

She swallowed. 'Again, that's up to you. If you decide you'd rather not go on, then just say so. And don't worry about me. It's separate, and I'm capable of keeping it that way. It's just a question of whether you are.'

'But what do you want?'

She met his eyes, but hers were so guarded he couldn't tell

what she was thinking. 'What do I want? I want you to do whatever you feel is right.'

'Then we keep it separate, and we carry on,' he told her, because the alternative, to lose that amazing vibrant warmth from his life, was too hard to contemplate.

She heard his pager bleeping at one twenty-five.

His bedroom was next to hers, just through the wall, and she could hear the soft murmur of his voice, then the sounds of him moving around.

And then she heard Freya cry, and his footsteps on the landing, and then his mother's voice remonstrating with him.

'I have to go!' he said, raising his voice so she could hear him clearly, then his mother replied, her voice tearful.

'James, I can't do this! She's getting so upset.'

'Mum, we've talked about this over and over again. I have to go to work.'

'James, please.'

Kate pulled on her dressing-gown and tapped on the communicating door. 'James? Let me in.'

It swung open, and he stood there, his eyes tormented, Freya in his arms, an older woman hovering in the background, twisting her hands.

'Give her to me,' Kate said, taking the baby from him. 'Now go. I'll join you later.'

'But—'

'No buts. Go.'

'I owe you.'

'I know.'

He sighed sharply, kissed Freya on the cheek and ran down the stairs. Seconds later the door banged behind him, and his car drove away, leaving them in silence.

'Right, sweetheart, let's get you back to bed,' she said to the gently grizzling Freya, and, kissing her soft, downy cheek, she tucked her back into her cot, covered her up and left her.

There was a little wail of protest, but nothing untoward, and she stood on the landing outside the partially open door and met James's mother's anguished eyes.

'You probably think I'm dreadful,' Mrs McEwan said unhappily.

'No. I think you're not very supportive of your son, but you obviously have your reasons for that, and they're none of my business. What is my business is getting him to work when he's meant to, so he can fulfil his contract, and I understood you had an agreement, so if you suddenly find you can't stick to that and you're going to let him down and make it even more difficult for him to keep his family intact, then I think that's somewhat unfair.'

'But I can't,' she said, and to Kate's complete astonishment, she started to cry.

'Come on, let's go and put the kettle on. You need to talk about this.' She put a hand on her shoulder and steered her towards the stairs, and once they were down in the kitchen she put the kettle on and settled back against the worktop while Mrs McEwan blew her nose and pulled herself together.

'Beth was so lovely. They were such a wonderful family,' she said unsteadily, 'and then this dreadful disease got hold of her and he just let her carry on with the baby, and if he hadn't, if he'd saved her—but they didn't even try, and now he wants me to support him, and I can't do it. I'm worried about my sister, and she wants me to spend time with her, and James needs me, and I can't deal with it on my own at night when he has to go. The responsibility just terrifies me, and I'm so afraid something dreadful will happen to one of them and it'll be my fault.'

'Right, let's take this one at a time,' Kate said gently but firmly, sitting her down at the kitchen table with a cup of tea.

'One, as I understand it, the cancer had already spread by the time Beth realised, and it was too late to save her, so whatever they'd done, it wouldn't have changed the outcome, it just would have given her more time. Probably only weeks, maybe months at best. And doing nothing, for the sake of Freya, was a very brave thing to do, and it must have torn James apart to sit there and watch it happen, knowing he was just going to lose her even sooner, but it was what she wanted, what she felt was right, and he supported her decision. I think that shows immense courage and fortitude, and you should be very proud of him.'

His mother stared at her, and then her eyes filled again. 'I am proud of him, but I can't be Beth.'

'He doesn't want you to be Beth. He wants you to be his mother, and you can do that. You can look after the children—you just need to be firmer. Freya doesn't miss her mother, she never knew her, and Rory's as good as gold. He sleeps through the night, he's happy and well adjusted—they really aren't a problem. They're a good family unit, and you really shouldn't try to undermine that because you haven't got the confidence to do what James is asking of you.'

'But I can't do it!'

'Then you need to tell him why. You need to tell him that you're afraid, and not tell him that he isn't in a position to keep his children, because losing them would destroy him, you know. He loves them so much, he's absolutely devoted to them, and he's only trying to do his job and maintain their quality of life. He's not trying to be unreasonable, but if you really are afraid to help him or too worried about your sister to feel able to give him the time he needs, then you need to explain that. I'm sure he'll understand, and he can make other arrangements, but it might take time. As long as he's here my parents are just over there in the farmhouse, and if you really couldn't cope, they'd give you a hand, but—Mrs McEwan, there's a permanent job coming up, and I think he should have it, but while there's this uncertainty hanging over him, I can't recommend him without reservation.'

Mrs McEwan stared at Kate for an age, then shook her head. 'I don't know what to do. I just know I can't.'

'What exactly are you afraid of?'

She huddled her arms around herself miserably. 'I don't know. What if the baby was sick and choked? Or got meningitis and I didn't realise? And what if Rory did something dangerous and fell or burnt himself or something? It's so silly,' she said, wringing her hands, 'but I feel like a new mother—that I don't know what to do, and I get so tired, but I don't know how to settle them if they wake.'

'Just be firm. Listen—what can you hear?'

There was absolute silence, apart from the ticking of the clock on the wall, and she stared at Kate.

'She's gone back to sleep!' she said, looking stunned.

'Of course she has. She had a busy day. She needs her sleep, and so do you. Don't pander to her, and she won't expect it.'

'That's what James always says.'

'Then maybe he has a point,' she said with a wry smile. 'She's his daughter, he's looked after her from day one. I think perhaps he knows her.' She lifted her head. 'That's my pager. It must be a big one. I'm going to have to go—will you be all right, Mrs McEwan, or do you want me to ring my mother? My parents are just over there, they won't mind.'

'No. No—I'll manage.'

'Look, I'll leave you the number so you can ring them if there's a problem, but I really don't think there will be,' she said, scribbling it on the back of an envelope. 'There. Call them if you need them.'

She nodded. 'Thank you, Kate. I'm sorry I've been such a nuisance. I really don't want to spoil his chances of a job, but—'

'Just talk to him. I have to go. Go back to bed and get some rest.'

She ran upstairs and through to her side, looked at her pager and dressed quickly. She was needed in Theatre, two victims of an RTA with internal injuries needing surgery, one of them pregnant, and James's mother would just have to cope.

He felt sick.

His mother was bottling out on him, he'd had to call Kate in because Jo didn't have enough experience to deal with the emergencies, and all he could see was Kate's implacable eyes when she'd taken Freya from him. If it hadn't been for her, he'd still be standing on the landing, arguing with his mother, and he just couldn't do it any more.

There was no way he could struggle through to the end of this contract, far less take the consultancy if he was offered it, and he felt gutted. He loved his work, he needed it. It was the only thing that kept him sane—apart from Kate—and after the fiasco on the landing that was no doubt all about to come to a crashing halt.

'What have we got?'

He gave a sigh of relief at the sound of her voice, calm and businesslike and in control. He met her eyes, and saw just cool caramel, and knew that it was all right. For now.

'Twenty-five-year-old male driver with ruptured diaphragm

and lacerated liver, and a twenty-six-year-old pregnant female passenger who's nearing term. I don't like the look of her at all, but there's nothing obvious and the ultrasound wasn't showing anything serious like a placental abruption. Yet. She's under observation and I've called for an obstetrician and got six units cross-matched to be on the safe side, but she might have splenic injuries. I'm not sure, but she's all right for now and the driver isn't, which is why I started on him— and he's got a fractured right radius and ulna as well that the orthos are going to deal with shortly.'

'OK. Can we have some music on, please? A nice bit of rock, I think.'

He met her calm, clear eyes. 'Rock?'

'Is that OK?'

He could have kissed her. 'That's fine.'

'Right, how far have you got?'

'I've clamped the liver to stop it bleeding. I'm just about to repair the diaphragm and then I'll go back to the liver and suture it properly.'

'OK, you lead, I'll assist, and when you're OK I'll go and see your pregnant lady.'

He nodded, put his child-care issues and the future of his career out his mind and concentrated on saving a young man's life.

'I don't like the look of her.'

'No. I agree. But is it abdominal or obstetric?'

He shrugged. 'I don't know. Where the hell is the obstetrician?'

'Pressure's dropping.'

'Kate, we've got to open her up and find out,' James said decisively, and she nodded.

'Want me to lead?'

'If you like.'

She didn't. Not really. It was the sort of situation where things could go wrong very fast, and although the baby's heartbeat was fine at the moment, she was very wary. Where *was* the obstetrician? 'We'd better call Obs again, and get a neonatal team standing by just in case. Are there any SCBU beds available?'

'I have no idea,' he muttered, scrubbing fast. 'This is ridiculous. Where are they?'

'I'll chase them up,' one of the theatre nurses said. Kate nodded. She was the only person who wasn't scrubbing or busy, and they didn't have time to waste. She was going downhill fast.

Faster than they'd realised, and when Kate opened her abdomen, there was nothing to indicate such a sudden deterioration.

'OK, she's got a ruptured spleen, but it's encapsulated, and there's no free blood in the abdomen. It must be obstetric,' she muttered.

'She's crashing,' the anaesthetist warned simultaneously, and James frowned, whipped back the drapes and swore.

'She's bleeding. She must have a placental abruption. We can't wait, I'll have to do a C-section. Can you stall the spleen?'

'Sure. Someone chase Obs and SCBU, please!' she snapped, and then a paediatrician came in, followed by a neonatal nurse pushing a crib.

'Thank God for small mercies. Suction!' James said, and Kate desperately tried to deal with the flood of blood and amniotic fluid as he opened the uterus and wriggled the baby free, passing it to the waiting paediatrician.

'Syntocinon!' he snapped. 'We're going to lose her if we can't get this bleeding stopped! Kate, deal with this.' And he handed her the placenta, grabbed a large pack and pressed it hard down on the inside of the uterine wall over the haemorrhage while the anaesthetist injected Syntocinon into her thigh to make her uterus contract.

Then a thin wail pierced the air, and he closed his eyes and laughed softly under his breath. 'Now, that's music to my ears,' he murmured, and, looking up, he met her eyes and smiled. 'So. That's one of them safe. Now, what's happening under here?'

He lifted the pack cautiously, and to their relief the site was just welling gently. As they watched, the uterus started contracting and the flow stopped completely. His shoulders dropped.

'OK. I think we're out of the woods, but I'll let the obstetrician check the placenta and close the uterus. Does anyone know where he is?'

'Delivering triplets, but he's nearly done. They're all out and fine. I'm in two places at once,' the paediatrician said with a wry grin. 'Still, this little chap looks good and he won't need me. We'll get him shipped up to SCBU and check him over thoroughly. Well done, guys. Not bad for a GS team.'

James snorted, but Kate couldn't keep the grin off her face.

There was no way she could have done that—well, not with his confidence. She hadn't done a C-section for years, and then only a few. He'd been fantastic—calm, decisive, confident.

He deserved that job—and if it was anything to do with her, she'd make sure he got it...

CHAPTER EIGHT

IT WAS like waiting for the other shoe to drop.

For three hours, she'd said nothing that wasn't directly connected to what they were doing, but now it was over, and he straightened up, walked away from the table and stripped off his gloves and gown and hat, chucking them in the bin as he passed.

He'd finished the driver alone while Kate checked the pregnant woman, then they'd left the driver with the orthopaedic surgeon and moved with the pregnant woman to the theatre next door, because there hadn't been time to wait.

And thank God they'd had that other theatre available.

She'd left him and the obstetrician closing and gone to check the driver in Recovery, and now everything was under control.

Except his private life.

'Good work, McEwan. That was…amazing.'

She was sitting in the staffroom, fingers curled around a mug of coffee, and he helped himself to one and sat down beside her, his head tipped back against the wall and his eyes closed, drained now that the adrenaline rush was over.

'I only did what anybody else would have done.'

'No. I couldn't have done it. I don't think I could have

remembered where to start—James, you were fantastic. You saved that baby's life—and the mother's.'

He turned his head and looked at her in astonishment, then smiled wryly. 'I've probably seen a C-section more recently than you, don't forget. Freya's only eighteen months old. And don't run away with the idea that I wasn't scared to death, because I was. Well, sort of. There wasn't a lot of time for that. Still, it worked, thankfully, and everything seems fine now. And I couldn't have done it alone, so thanks for coming in.'

She smiled, her eyes warm and approving. 'My pleasure. I haven't had so much excitement in years, and I wouldn't have missed it for the world.'

He grunted and sat up, taking a long slug of coffee and sighing before meeting her eyes again. 'Look—I'm sorry about earlier. I'm going to have to do something about this.'

Her smiled faded and she pressed her lips together and nodded. 'You are. You need to talk to your mother. She's scared of the responsibility, you know.'

He stared at her incredulously, unable to believe his ears. 'What?'

'You heard. She's worried there'll be an emergency and she won't know what to do, and she's frightened she won't cope alone.'

He closed his eyes and dragged his free hand over his face. 'Oh, that's crazy. She can't be serious.'

'She is—deadly serious. It's not you she thinks can't look after the children, it's her, and she doesn't know how to tell you.'

'Is that what this is all about? Good grief. So how was she when you handed Freya back to her and went out?'

'Fine—and I didn't hand Freya back to her, I put her back

to bed and she went straight to sleep. She whinged for about a minute, tops, and your mother was amazed.'

He laughed, unable to believe it. 'Just like that? How did you know that? I mean, I know that, but she's my daughter. You don't do kids. You're too busy ticking your boxes.'

She gave a wry laugh. 'That's what you think. I've been brought up with random children arriving in the house from who knows what kind of circumstances for almost my entire life, and getting kids back to sleep when they wake in the night is second nature to me. And the only thing wrong with Freya was that she'd been disturbed and wanted to go back to sleep.'

He shook his head in disbelief. 'You're a marvel. I leave you alone with my family for five minutes and you've got them all sorted out. I should hire you.'

'In your dreams, McEwan,' she said drily, and he snorted.

She was in his dreams, all right. In his dreams, in his thoughts, in his arms. She was so deeply enmeshed in his life he couldn't imagine what he'd do without her. He put that out of his mind and turned towards her. 'So—what do I do about my mother, oh wise one?'

'Well, I left her with my parents' phone number in case of emergencies, but she really isn't confident. Which is silly, because I'm sure she's perfectly capable. She brought you up, didn't she, and you survived.'

'Mmm. Maybe that's the trouble,' he murmured. 'I was a horror. Rory's a total angel compared to me. If there was something to climb, I was up it, and if there was something dirty or muddy, I was in it. By the time I was five I'd broken both arms, been in hospital with concussion and nearly killed myself falling down a cliff. And I took everything to bits. I took the iron to bits when I was six and turned it on to see how it worked, and set fire to the ironing board. It's a miracle no one was killed. They got me a really complicated construction set after that to keep my fingers out of mischief, and enrolled me in the Cubs. At least it gave them one night a week when they didn't have to worry.'

'Poor woman,' she said, smiling sympathetically. 'No wonder she's so stressed. You've damaged her for life.'

'I'd better ring her—apologise for yelling at her.'

'It might be an idea. And you need to sit down and have a nice long chat and see where you go from here, because I really think she'll struggle to have them for a whole weekend—and we're on this weekend. And, no, I can't manage without you. You've seen the sort of thing that can go wrong, and Jo just hasn't got the experience to handle it.'

His relief evaporated, and with a heavy sigh he got to his feet. 'I hadn't forgotten. Don't worry, Kate, I'll sort something out—get some back-up of some sort. Maybe Helen can have them. And in the New Year I'll get a nanny. I want that job— and I intend to get it, if there's the slightest chance. So I will get it sorted. Properly.'

She studied him in silence for a moment, then gave him an enigmatic smile. 'I know you will. Now, go and ring her, and I'll check the post-ops again, and then we'd better go and get ready for the day.'

After the events of the night, the day was relatively peaceful.

Their two RTA victims were doing well and had met their new baby, and when he went up to check on them, they were both highly emotional and almost embarrassingly grateful.

'Thank you so much. I don't know what I would have done if I'd lost them both,' the driver whispered unsteadily.

'My pleasure. You just concentrate on getting better and enjoying the baby.'

He left them to it and went to see Tracy, and found her sitting up in her chair looking hugely better.

'Hey! Nice haircut. You look fabulous,' he said, sitting down on the edge of her bed and admiring the short, choppy style—a much safer choice for someone with trichophagia, and the first line of defence, usually, so he wasn't surprised to see it.

She touched it self-consciously, but she looked pleased. 'I'm going to have it coloured. Mum said I can have high-lights, but I want to do it purple.'

He laughed. 'Well, it's your hair, but are you sure purple would suit you? You're quite pale. The highlights might look more sophisticated, but you've got to do what makes you feel best.'

'You think highlights?'

'Whatever. It's not my hair, but the good thing about it is, whatever you do, it'll grow out. How are you otherwise?'

'Better. My stomach's stopped hurting, and I can eat now, just sloppy stuff, but I'm so hungry. I haven't really been eating for ages, and Mum says I need to catch up.'

'You do, but take it easy and don't have too much at once for a while. Let your stomach heal, and you need to keep taking the pills to stop your stomach acid from damaging the wall until it's healed properly. The dietician will give you a list of things to avoid for a while, but you need to play it by ear and only eat the things that don't upset you. Apart from that, as far as I'm concerned you're doing really well, and the mental health team are happy to treat you as an outpatient, so you could go home today or tomorrow if you feel ready.' He hesitated, then said, 'Any word from your boyfriend?'

She shook her head. 'My friend said he's really sad.'

'Then maybe you need to ring him—or give me his number. Let me talk to him.'

She scribbled it on a piece of paper, and he put it in his pocket and stood up. 'You take care—and I want to see the hair when you come back to Outpatients for a check-up.'

He went back to Kate's office and rang the number, but it went straight to the answering machine. Lessons, he thought, realising that the lad was still at school. He'd try him later. He couldn't get his mother, either, so she'd probably gone to Cambridge to visit her sister.

Which meant there was nothing for it but paperwork—starting with Tracy's discharge.

'Kate?'

'James, hi. Are you OK?'

His laugh sounded a little off-kilter, and she sat up straighter. 'What's happened?'

'Um—you know that car you had, that was like my life? Well, another bit just fell off it. Are you busy?'

'No-o,' she said cautiously. 'Why?'

'Because I've been a complete idiot, and I'm stuck. I put petrol in my car.'

'So?'

'It's a diesel car.'

'Ah.'

'So it has to go to the garage and be pumped out and rinsed through and decontaminated and filters and fuel lines and stuff changed, and it's going to cost a fortune, and I really don't need it right now, and I'm sitting in it with the kids waiting for the recovery truck to come and get me, and

Freya's crying and Rory's hungry and this is going to take ages and I just want to *scream*, really. And I hate to ask, but...'

She laughed, even though it wasn't funny. 'OK, where are you?' she asked, standing up and wriggling her feet into her shoes.

'On the road out to you, just off the bypass. You can't miss us.'

'Give me five minutes.'

She was there in four, and, sure enough, he was standing by the car waiting for her, arms folded over his chest and looking thoroughly disgusted.

'You're a star. I can't believe I was such an idiot.'

'I'm sure it's easily done,' she said. 'Right, kids, come on, let's go home and have some tea while your daddy sorts out his muddle, shall we?'

And scooping up the baby's bag and Rory's booster seat, she installed him in her car while James sorted out Freya and her seat, then she looked at him over the roof. 'I'll see you at home whenever. Don't worry about them, I'll get them into bed if you're still not back—and I'll cook for you.'

His shoulders drooped with relief. 'Thanks. I owe you.'

'Again?' she teased, and, getting into her car, she drove home.

'So what were you doing at school today?' she asked Rory while she loaded the dishwasher.

'Christmas stuff,' he said, little legs swinging under the kitchen table. 'We made cards and angels and things and hung them on the tree.' He put his head on one side and rested it on his hand, studying her earnestly. 'Will you help me write a letter to Father Christmas? You said you would.'

'Yes, sure. It sounds as if Freya's asleep, so we can do it now. Stay here, I'll get some paper.'

She slipped through to her side of the house and went back armed with a sheaf of coloured paper and some pencils, and settled herself down beside him.

'You'd better kneel up so you can reach,' she said, and put some paper in front of him. 'Right, what do you want to say?'

'Dear Father Christmas.'

Well, that was easy. 'Dear Father Christmas,' she repeated slowly as she wrote it out nice and clearly on a separate sheet. 'Right, you copy that, and we'll do the next bit.'

She watched him, his tongue sticking out of the side of his mouth in concentration, and she was sure if she could see behind James's mask when he was operating, he'd be doing the same. It made her smile, and Rory looked up at her and grinned.

'There. Done it. Now "I want".'

'Don't you think it should be, "Please may I have"?' she suggested, and he nodded.

'OK,' she said, and wrote 'Please may I have' on the sheet he was copying from, then turned to him. 'Have what? What do you want to say now?'

'A mummy for Christmas.'

Her heart jammed in her throat, and she felt her eyes fill. 'Oh, Rory, sweetheart—I don't think Father Christmas does mummies,' she said gently, her heart breaking. 'I think he only does toys and stuff like that.'

His face fell, that wonderful sparkle in his eyes dying right away and taking her heart with it. 'But I don't want toys,' he said, sounding bewildered and unbearably disappointed. 'I've got toys. I want a mummy. Grandma always says Freya misses her mummy, and I thought, if we had a mummy, then Freya wouldn't cry when Daddy goes to work and Grandma wouldn't get upset and cry, too, and everybody would be happy, and Daddy wouldn't cry any more. I hear him at night, sometimes, when he thinks we're sleeping, and I hate it.'

'Oh, darling.' She wrapped her arms round him and gave him a hug, and he snuggled into her and stayed there for ages, his face buried in her chest, his little knees pushed up against the sides of her thighs while she rested her cheek against his hair and rubbed his back gently and thought of James crying in the night, and she had to blink the tears away.

She could be his mummy, she thought longingly. She'd love to be his mummy, and Freya's, and live with them and James, and be happy ever after…

She heard a car pull up, and lifted her head. 'That sounds like your daddy now,' she said, and he sat up away from her and stared at the paper.

'I don't want to write to Father Christmas any more,' he said, getting down and screwing up the letter and throwing it at the bin. 'He's rubbish.'

And without another word, he ran away upstairs and went into his room, banging the door shut.

'Hi. I'm sorry I've been so long, but I had to sort out a hire car. Everything all right?'

Kate was sitting at his kitchen table smoothing out a sheet of paper, her eyes anguished, and he felt a sudden flicker of dread.

'What? What is it?'

'We were writing to Father Christmas,' she said, her voice hollow.

He glanced down at the table. 'Dear Father Christmas, please may I have,' he read in Rory's shaky script, the paper crumpled and torn. He looked up at Kate. 'Have what?'

'A mummy for Christmas,' she said, and closed her eyes. A tear slid down her cheek, and he sighed sharply and rammed his hands through his hair.

Whatever next?

'I can't give him a mummy,' he said desperately, his voice cracking. 'They don't just grow on trees. What does he want me to do, get a mail-order bride?' His voice cracked again, and he slammed his fist down on the worktop. Damn. Damn, damn, damn.

'So what did you say to him?'

'I told him Father Christmas only does toys, so he said he's rubbish and ran up to bed. James, I'm so sorry. I didn't know what to say to him.' She scrubbed away the tear with her fingertips, but it was joined by another one and he went over to her and rested his hand on her shoulder.

'Don't cry,' he said gruffly. 'It isn't your fault. I'll go and talk to him.' He dragged in a breath. 'Where's Freya?'

'Asleep.'

Thank God for small mercies, he thought. Leaving Kate there, he ran upstairs and went into Rory's room and found him in a huddle in his bed, Beth's teddy clutched against his chest, sobbing his heart out. 'Hey, come on, where's my brave boy gone?' he asked softly, gathering him into his arms.

'I just wanted a mummy,' he said, and James felt his heart break all over again.

'I know, but we can't always have what we want, and we've got each other and Freya, and we can be happy, Rory. We can. We don't need Father Christmas for that.'

He wasn't sure if he was saying it to his son or to himself, but if saying it could make it true, he'd say it over and over and over again. He lay down beside Rory and pulled him closer, and he snuggled up tight and gradually his little chest stopped hiccuping with sobs and he drifted into sleep.

James didn't. He lay there, emotionally drained and physically exhausted, and wondered when they'd ever get out of the dark tunnel that seemed to be going on for ever.

A light touch on his shoulder startled him, and he turned his head to find Kate looking down at him, her eyes shadowed.

'Are you OK?' she whispered, and he nodded.

'He's asleep. I'll come down.'

He got up off the bed, tucked Rory in and followed Kate down to the kitchen. There was a wonderful smell drifting from the hob, and she'd laid the table.

Like a normal family, he thought a trifle hysterically, and had to stop the runaway thought in its tracks.

'It's only spaghetti sauce that I had in the freezer, and I've got some fresh pasta. I'll cook it now, if you're hungry?'

'Starving,' he confessed. Dropping into a chair, he propped his chin on his hands and sighed. 'What a mess. The house, the car, and now this. When's it going to end, Kate?'

She poured boiling water into a pan, dropped in the pasta and sat down opposite him, sliding a glass of wine across the table to him. 'James, don't give up. You're getting there. It's just because it's Christmas. It's always hard on families in your situation, but it'll soon be next year, and things will pick up.'

'Will they? I need that job, Kate,' he told her, and he could hear the desperation in his voice, but he was powerless to do anything about it. 'I have to work. It's the only thing that keeps me sane and grounded, the only thing I seem to be able to do well.'

'That's rubbish!' she exclaimed. 'You're a wonderful father, James. I've seen you with your children, and you adore them, and they adore you. You're really close, and yet they're normal, well-balanced children.'

'Not according to my mother,' he said.

'Your mother's struggling, James. She's lost her husband, her sister's lost her husband, you've lost your wife—she's going through a bad time, and she's terrified she's going to make it worse by something that she does or doesn't do. She doesn't really think you should give them up, she's just worried for you all and can't see a way out.'

'She's not alone, but we'll get there, you're right. I just need to sort the kids out with some better arrangement.'

'What about asking Helen?' she suggested. 'Maybe she could have them to stay?'

He shook his head. 'I've tried that. She won't. Her husband doesn't mind her looking after other people's children during the day, but at night he draws the line, and I can understand that. It doesn't help me, but I understand it. I think the only answer is a nanny, but I can't get one this close to Christmas—even if I had anywhere to house one. How's the pasta doing?'

'Oh!' She leapt up, drained it and sighed with relief. 'I think it's OK still. Sorry. Right—parmesan?'

He needed that job.

If ever a man needed a future to look forward to, that man was James.

He didn't make love to Kate that night, just sat with her on the sofa for an hour and then kissed her goodnight at her door. And she'd thought they'd moved beyond that. He hadn't worn his wedding ring since the night of the wedding party, and she'd foolishly allowed herself to attach some significance to it.

Stupid. Clearly there was no significance to it. Maybe he'd just lost it, but, whatever the reason, he wasn't with her tonight. She guessed he was too raw, and Rory's plea to Father Christmas must have brought thoughts of Beth back to the surface.

Damn. Well, she'd known in her heart he was still grieving for her, she'd known it wasn't for ever, but she still felt ludicrously lonely with the bed to herself. Still, that was her problem. Getting the job was his, and if there was a way she could make it work for him, then she had to try it, for all their sakes.

The following night she went over to see her mother while James was putting the children to bed and talking to his mother. 'How do you fancy a job?' she asked, and her mother laughed.

'I don't. Why?'

'I just need James to have reliable child care, and for that he needs a nanny. You must know someone. I wondered if you wanted to come up with a shortlist of people you'd trust.'

She laughed again. 'It would be a short list.'

'Please try.'

'OK. I will. Is this about the new consultant's post?'

Kate nodded. 'I can't put him forward for it until he's sorted, but he needs it so desperately. He's sad, and Rory—' She broke off, and her mother tipped her head on one side.

'Rory?'

So she told Sue about the letter, and her mother clicked her tongue sympathetically. 'Poor little mite. Of course, you could solve the problem at a stroke.'

'How?'

'By volunteering.'

'For what? To be his nanny?'

'No. To be his wife.'

She sat back abruptly. 'His— Mum, you're being ridiculous. He doesn't want another wife. He's still grieving for the first one.'

'Is he? When you came back from the wedding he didn't look to me like a man who was grieving for his wife.'

Damn. Her mother saw too much.

'It's just physical,' she said, looking down at the table and chasing a few grains of salt around with her fingertip. 'I know it's not going anywhere.'

'But you'd like it to.'

'I don't know,' she lied, because she couldn't bear to admit out loud just how much she loved them all, how much he'd fallen for a man and a family wrapped in grief, and how much her heart was breaking every day…

'I spoke to Tracy's boyfriend yesterday,' James said as they paused in a break in their clinic the following morning. 'He said he really missed her, but he just felt sick whenever he thought about it. I suggested he go along with her to see her counsellor, because he's part of her problem, really. If stress is triggering it, and breaking up with him is stressing her, it won't help her at all.'

'And?'

'He's going to talk to her. They're only very young, but they seem to care about each other quite genuinely. We'll have to wait and see. I've done what I can, and at least he's prepared to talk to her now.'

Kate smiled at him, her eyes warm, like caramel. Not toffee. Not any more. The sharp shards seemed to be gone, and the warmth gave him hope. 'Well done,' she said, and he felt a glow inside.

Crazy. She wasn't interested. She'd gone over to her parents' last night, and after his mother had gone he'd hoped she'd come through to see him, but she hadn't, and he'd ended up going to bed and reading and wishing he was with her.

Of course he could have tapped on the door himself, but since she'd told him on Monday that she couldn't recommend him for the job without reservation because of his child-care issues, she hadn't been near him. Well, not in that way.

And he missed her. Stupid.

And stupid, of course, for having suggested to her that she might not want to have such a close relationship with him. If he hadn't done that, then she might have come in last night, but maybe not. It put her in a difficult position, after all, if the hospital board was going to be asking her what she thought of him and they were involved to that extent in their personal lives.

Involved?

Was that really the word for the most amazing, astonishing, mind-blowing sex—no, scratch that, relationship—he'd ever had in his life? Hell. He'd loved Beth to bits, but they'd never had what he had with Kate. He'd never felt that he'd die if he couldn't hold her, that the day was colourless if he couldn't be with her, that the nights were endless...

'How did you get on with your mother?' she asked, bringing him slamming back down to earth, and he scrubbed a hand through his hair and shrugged.

'OK. We had a long talk, and she's not really happy.'

'But she will do the weekend?'

He nodded. 'Yes, she'll do the weekend. She did mention your parents as back-up—will they be there?'

'Yes, of course, and they won't mind at all. And if it all goes haywire, I'm sure Mum will step in.'

He felt a wave of relief, but it was short-lived. She couldn't support him for the consultancy if her family was having to pick up the pieces, and—

'Hey, cheer up, it might never happen,' she said, grinning at him. 'What are you doing this evening?'

He stared at her. 'This evening? I have no idea.'

'Done your Christmas shopping?'

He must have looked blank, because she laughed and rolled her eyes. 'Men. It's Thursday—late-night shopping, the last before Christmas Day, which is next Thursday, a week today, in case you've managed to miss that. Want to go to town?'

'What about the children?'

'Bring them. They'll love it. We've only got a clinic, we can be away by five-thirty if we're lucky. You can buy them supper in town, and they can go on the roundabout and see the carol singers and the Christmas lights. Go on, it'll be fun!'

Christmas.

A week today.

Fun?

'OK,' he said, a little dumbfounded, but for the rest of the day it was all he could think of.

CHAPTER NINE

THE children came alive.

She'd never seen them like that, and it was wonderful. Rory was so excited he could hardly speak, and little Freya in her buggy had eyes like saucers.

'What's that music?' Rory asked, his head cocked on one side, and James lifted him up and pointed down the street.

'The Salvation Army band and choir. They're playing Christmas carols.'

'Me see!' Freya shrieked, and he lifted her up, too, so she could see them.

'Why don't we get closer?' Kate suggested, and they threaded their way through the crowd, James holding Rory by the hand and Kate pushing the buggy, and it suddenly occurred to her that to an outsider they'd look just like any other family.

If only.

James lifted Freya up onto her shoulders, then hoisted Rory up onto his, and they watched the Salvation Army until Freya became restless. 'Shall we go and do some shopping, then?' James suggested, and as they turned away, he dropped some money in the collecting tin.

'I want to give them some,' Rory said, struggling to get

down, so James gave him a few coins, and then Freya wanted to do it, and by the time they got away his pockets were all but empty.

'So much for my car-park money,' he said drily, but Kate had a purse full of change so it wasn't an issue.

'How about the roundabout?' she suggested, and Rory tipped his head and looked up at her.

'Is it like the one at the park?' he asked.

'Sort of, I expect—there's one here with music and lights and things, like a fairground ride.'

'Wow! What's a fairground?' he asked.

'Why don't we have a look?' James suggested, so they did.

Rory's eyes boggled. 'Wow! I want to go on it.'

'Me go!' Freya yelled, struggling to get out of the buggy, and then cried when the man said she wasn't big enough.

'Sorry, darlin',' he said kindly. 'Why doesn't your mum put you on that one?'

Her mum?

Oh, Lord. Trying hard to remember how to breathe, she gave James a shrug, and led Freya across the cobbles to the other ride. It was a tiny roundabout, with little carriages set in a circle, pushed by an elderly woman with a big warm smile, and she tucked Freya in, fastened her straps and pushed her gently round while she shrieked and giggled with delight.

And Kate stood and smiled at her and wondered what it would be like to have the right to be called her mother…

Hell. She'd looked horrified, and then she'd shrugged dismissively and walked away, leaving him with a great lump in his throat and a huge *I wish* that wouldn't go away.

But was that what he really wanted? Kate, as the children's new mother?

Rory's mummy for Christmas?

Ludicrous. She wouldn't have him, so there was no point suggesting it. She'd made her feelings on the subject quite clear when he'd suggested jokingly that she should be their nanny. *In your dreams*, she'd said with a wealth of feeling, and although he knew she was fond of the kids, there was no way she was going to be interested in taking them on. Even she wasn't that soft.

The ride came to an end, and he held out his hand to a thoroughly over-excited Rory, bubbling like champagne, and went to find the woman who was beginning to haunt not only his dreams but every waking hour as well.

'OK?'

'Again!' Freya demanded, but James shook his head and lifted her out, and they headed up to the shops.

'Do you have a list?' Kate asked him, ever practical, and of course he didn't.

'I need something for my mother,' he said, utterly at a loss because out of the blue now he felt he didn't know her at all.

'Get her something pretty,' Kate suggested. 'She's having a hard time. Spoil her a bit. How about a pamper day?'

'A pamper day?'

Kate laughed. 'You don't have to say it as if it's toxic!' she said, and he chuckled wryly.

'Sorry. I would just never have thought of giving my mother that sort of thing.'

'Maybe because you've never really thought of her as a woman, just as your mother,' she said.

Was that true? He realised that it probably was. And while he was on the subject of his mother, he also realised that he probably hadn't given her a choice about helping him, and he'd been so tied up in his own grief and misery he'd utterly failed to notice hers. She'd lost his father only four years before Beth had died, and he'd been so tied up with his new job and his new wife and his new house that he hadn't really been there for her.

And then she'd had to support him through his own grief, and now her sister was widowed and ill, and he was expecting her to drop everything and deal with a stroppy toddler and an active little boy so he could carry on with his life.

So what kind of a son did that make him?

Selfish and unthinking, he decided, and it didn't taste good.

He bought her a pamper day, as Kate had suggested, and some smellies, and then she took the children off so he could find them a few presents. He also wanted to get something for Kate, and then he saw a pretty little jumper very like her favourite. His favourite, too, and she'd said only the other day that it had a hole in it. This one might be just the thing to replace it.

He didn't even look at the price. He owed her so much that the price was irrelevant and, anyway, he found he was enjoying it. It was such a long time since shopping had been more than a chore, and he was getting into his stride. He found another jumper which he thought would suit his mother—Kate had said get her something pretty, so he did, and he picked up all sorts of little bits and pieces for the children—stockings to hang under the tree, and all manner of things to fill them, and a wooden jigsaw for Freya and a train set for Rory—not the mother he'd asked for, but there was nothing he could do about that, he thought bleakly, and then caught sight of Kate's dark head in the crowd and felt his heart squeeze.

If only…

'I'm shattered,' he said with a groan, unloading the car after he'd brought the children in and got them off to bed.

Kate laughed and eased her shoes off. 'Me, too. It's surprising how much more tiring it is when you've got to keep an eye on a toddler. I'd forgotten. It's a while since I've helped Mum with little ones. I think they had fun, though, don't you?'

'Yes, I'm sure they did, and it's all thanks to you. It was a great idea.'

He hung the bags full of presents in the under-stairs cupboard, out of reach, and turned back to her. 'Fancy a cup of tea?'

'I'd love one. I'm parched. I'll make it.'

She filled the kettle and put it on, and then glanced up at the window and saw him watching her reflection. The light wasn't good enough to read his expression, but there was a curious stillness about him. She turned round slowly and met his eyes.

'What's the matter?' she asked softly, and if she hadn't been watching him so carefully she would have missed the shrug.

'Nothing. I was just thinking how much difference you've made to our lives.'

'Oh, James.'

She didn't know why he'd kept his distance—because she'd said what she had about his child care being unreliable? Probably, and he'd seemed to imply that he wanted a little space between them, although he'd suggested in the end that they should keep work separate and carry on as they were, but they hadn't. Because of circumstances getting in the way, or because she'd destroyed something special between them?

She didn't know, but she couldn't let him stand there in the middle of the kitchen with that rather lost look in his eyes without giving him a hug.

She slid her arms round him, and after a second she felt his arms close around her and his head come down, his cheek resting against her hair.

'Thank you for tonight,' he murmured. 'It's really been fun. I wouldn't have thought of taking the children Christmas shopping if you hadn't suggested it, and they've really had a ball.'

He sighed, and she tipped her head back and stared into his eyes. 'What is it?'

'Oh, my mother. It occurred to me when you suggested I didn't think of her as a woman that I probably hadn't so much asked as told her she was helping me with the kids so I could get back to work. And I'd never asked her about her feelings or if she felt up to it. I just made her promise to help me, and I shouldn't have done.'

'So what are you going to do?'

'I don't know. Find an alternative, certainly, but what? Got any suggestions?'

'I might have. I asked Mum to think about it and see if she could come up with anyone.'

'And has she?'

'Not that she's mentioned yet, but when I asked her to draw up a shortlist, she said it would be.'

He chuckled, his eyes crinkling at the corners and softening the bleak expression they wore all too often. Then the crinkles faded, replaced by an unspoken question, and she went up on tiptoe and pressed her lips to his.

'Do you really want tea?' she said, and held her breath.

The corner of his mouth tugged down with irony. 'Tea?' he said softly. 'I don't think so. I think the only thing I really want is you.'

She stared up at him as his eyes darkened, wondering if

she was reading more into his words than she should. Yes. Of course she was. She was simply a diversion, something good to take the edge off his loneliness, a physical release that helped him deal with his emotional stress.

He didn't really want her. Not like that.

She stepped back and held out her hand. 'Ditto,' she said with a smile, and led him through the connecting door to her house.

He had two hours off at the end of Friday afternoon, and he collected Freya and his mother and took them to see Rory in his school nativity play. He was a shepherd, and when Freya saw him she shrieked and giggled and pointed, and James cuddled her on his lap and shushed her, but nobody minded.

And his mother really seemed to enjoy it.

He was looking at her through different eyes, he realised, and for the first time in ages, he gave her a hug as they came out of the hall and got their refreshments and waited for Rory to join them.

'That was such fun,' she said wistfully. 'I haven't been to a nativity play since you were tiny.'

'That's a long time ago.'

'It is. Decades.' She smiled up at him. 'Rory was lovely.'

He grinned, full of paternal pride. 'He was. He's a great little guy—and here he is. Hello, tiger.'

'Hi—hello, Grandma! Did you see me?'

'We all saw you—didn't you hear Freya calling you?'

He giggled. 'She's naughty.'

'No, she was just excited,' he said. 'Shall we go home, then? Where are your things?'

'Here,' he said, holding up a carrier bag stuffed with paintings and a shoebag with a sock hanging out of it.

James rescued the sock, took the carrier bag from him and led them out to the car. He had to drop them off, and then he was due back at work. He just hoped the weekend went without a hitch.

Sue still hadn't come up with any solutions, and his mother had agreed to cover for him on the understanding that Kate's parents would help her out if necessary, but before he could go back to work that evening he needed to take them home and get them settled and introduce his mother to Sue so she was reassured.

He couldn't believe it had never occurred to him that she'd be apprehensive, and he felt so guilty.

They'd have to have a long heart to heart at some point, but for now, he just gave her a hug as he left to go back to work. 'I'm really sorry I've put you in this position,' he said softly. 'I feel awful asking you to do it, but it's the last time, I promise. I'll find someone else.'

'Don't be silly,' she said, trying to sound brave and failing. 'We'll be all right. As you said, they aren't little hellions like you were.'

He grinned a little off-kilter. 'No. That would be a nightmare.'

She chuckled and pushed him towards the door. 'Go on, go to work. Sue's promised to give me a hand if I need it, and I'm sure I'll be all right.'

He hoped so, because the last thing he needed was any more screw-ups. He'd spent last night with Kate—or the early part of it, anyway—and it had been amazing. Again. Neither of them had mentioned work or children or anything remotely contentious, and it had been bliss. And now they were going to be working together all weekend, and he found he was looking forward to that, too.

OK, it was the weekend before Christmas, the height of the party season and prime time for accidents and hernias and intestinal disasters, but he loved it. He thrived on it, and the busier, the better.

And it was busy.

By the time he got back, Kate was in Theatre with a strangulated hernia in a man who'd tried to carry too much shopping in out of the car, and no sooner had he scrubbed to assist than he had to go down to A and E.

'What have you got for me?' he asked, and Tom looked at him and sighed.

'It would be Kate's team on take this weekend, wouldn't it?' he said under his breath.

'Why?'

'Because it's her ex-husband.'

He frowned. 'Jon? He always goes private, she said.'

'Not when his car's been involved in a collision and he's got suspected internal injuries,' Tom said drily.

'Well, I'll have to deal with him. Where is he?'

'In Resus. He's stable, but he's definitely in pain, so we're monitoring him closely. He's booked for CT shortly.'

'Any clues?'

Tom pursed his lips. 'Might be spleen. He was driving, and there's some evidence of a seat-belt injury across the upper left quadrant. That would be consistent with spleen, and I've just got a feeling about it. It certainly doesn't look like his aorta.'

'Good. I don't need that and I don't suppose he does. Have we got an ultrasound machine down here?'

'Yeah, there's one in Resus you can use. It's not brilliant. I couldn't see anything a few minutes ago, but if it's got worse it might show now.'

James went into Resus and found Jon Burgess restless, in pain and, if his guess was correct, a little frightened.

'Hi, Jon. I'm James—we met at the wedding. How are you doing?' he asked, finding a professional smile from somewhere.

'James? Kate's friend?'

'That's right. Tell me how you're feeling.'

'Sore. Really very sore, and it's getting worse.'

'Can you point to it?' he asked, turning back the blanket, and Jon indicated an area covered by a mottled bruise. 'OK. I want to do another ultrasound scan of the area. It may hurt a little when I press, but if it gets too much, just tell me.'

Jon grunted when he ran the ultrasound head over the bruise, but James had seen enough. There was a large mass behind the spleen, and he was convinced he had an encapsulated haemorrhage. And if the membrane tore...

'Jon, you're going to need urgent surgery,' he said, not bothering to beat about the bush. 'I think you've ruptured your spleen.'

'Are you sure about that? You know what you're looking for with that stupid machine? There were just a load of lines and blotches. A better one—'

'I'm sure,' he said. 'As sure as I can be—and, yes, I know what I'm looking for. I don't think there's any point in waiting for a CT scan, I'd rather get you up to Theatre now. Kate's just finishing off, so we won't keep you long.'

'I don't want Kate doing it!' he said hastily. 'I mean, I'm sure she's perfectly competent, but—'

'Kate won't be doing it,' he told him firmly. 'I will. I need you to sign a consent form, and then we'll get you straight up to Theatre.'

'I hope it'll be thoroughly sterilised! I don't want any

hospital superbugs,' he said, but then the seriousness of his situation began to dawn on him, and panic filled his eyes. 'Um—if I give you a number, could you ring someone for me? Her name's Julia.'

'Sure.'

He took the number, got the consent form signed and then went and broke the news to Kate.

'Jon?' she said, looking stunned. 'Oh, Lord. Is he all right?'

He grinned. 'Well, he's talking about superbugs, so I don't think he's that near the brink. It's his spleen—should be straightforward.' He handed her the number. 'Here. Can you ring this lady for him? I think it's your ex's latest conquest.'

She stared at it, surprise on her face. 'No, it's his mother. They haven't spoken for years, but she was at the wedding, of course. I'll call her. She's a darling. And—James?'

He met her eyes questioningly.

'Take care of him. Don't give him too big an incision. He'll hate the scar.'

Like he would have hated hers? He felt his mouth tighten. 'Of course I'll take care of him. He's a patient, first and foremost.' Even if he was cruel and insensitive and stupid and had made Kate feel bad about herself. And he'd do his best not to split him open from end to end, however tempting.

He went and scrubbed.

'Busy weekend?' Sue asked Kate on Saturday afternoon when she managed to slip home for a while.

'Dire. Jon's in. He had a car accident and ruptured his spleen. James operated while I phoned his mother and broke the news.'

'Good heavens. Is he all right?'

'Oh, yes. He's in a side room, complaining about the service and driving all the nurses mad, apparently. We're obviously giving him too much pain relief. I'll have to get James to reduce it.'

Her mother frowned at her. 'Kate, that's not funny.'

'Oh, Mum, lighten up. James has much too much integrity to do anything like that, and so have I. You should know that.'

'I just know what Jon did to you.'

'It was years ago,' she said, and realised that it was, and for the first time, it really felt like it. She yawned and stretched, and looked hopefully into the fridge. 'Is there any food I can raid?' she asked, and her mother moved the kettle off the Aga and headed for the larder.

'A bowl of Saturday soup, and some fruit cake?'

'Fantastic. And a cup of tea, and then I'll have to dash. I'm taking it in turns with James to come home, and he's got to tuck the children up for the night, so I mustn't make him late. How's his mother coping?'

'Marion? She's fine. We've had a wonderful day. We took the children for a walk to feed the ducks, and they joined us for lunch, and it was lovely. She's a nice woman. Very nice.'

'She is a nice woman. She just can't cope, and I find that really odd. I suppose I'm spoilt, because you can cope with anything.'

Sue smiled wryly. 'Oh, no, I can't. I nearly went to pieces when I saw you in hospital after that idiot kicked you.'

'But you didn't. That's the thing. And you never do.'

'Horses for courses. I can do children. Do you ever go to pieces when you're faced with a difficult operation?'

'No, because it wouldn't help.'

'So how would it help in a domestic situation?' she asked with her usual common sense, and Kate just laughed.

'OK, you win, we're all good at something. So what's Marion good at?'

'Playing with them. She's marvellous. She just lacks confidence, but today she really enjoyed herself. I don't think she's got a problem at all, you know, I think if she could get back her confidence she'd be in her element. She's just out of practice. I think you should back James for this job. It could be just what he needs. Well, apart from a wife, and you know what I think about that.'

The microwave pinged, and Kate rescued her soup, sat down at the table and didn't answer.

But that didn't mean she wasn't thinking about it, because she was, all the time. It was how to put the idea into his head that was the tricky bit…

They got through the weekend without any major dramas, and handed over their patients on Monday afternoon to another team. He and Kate had Tuesday and Christmas Day off, and Sue and Andrew were having the children for him with the family on Boxing Day, but Helen was having them on Christmas Eve, so he went straight over there and retrieved them as soon as he was finished, to give her a little time off.

'Can we have a Christmas tree?' Rory asked excitedly on the way home. 'Helen's got a tree. It's really nice.'

'I expect so. We haven't got any decorations, though.' None at all. He'd thrown them all out in a fit of despair last Christmas, when he'd been packing up the London house, and he hadn't got round to replacing them. Now, suddenly, he found he wanted to put up a tree and decorate it with his children. 'Let's go and ask Kate's mother where we should get everything from,' he said, and they went home and found Sue and Andrew in the farmyard, struggling with a huge spruce.

'Good grief—Andrew, let me give you a hand,' he said, and

Sue surrendered her end and took charge of the children while they struggled into the high-ceilinged hall and jammed it upright in a great big bucket of sand.

'I was going to ask you where we could get a tree,' he said a little faintly, 'but I don't think we need one that big!'

Sue laughed. 'I've put one in the barn already. I hope you don't mind, but with the others coming—well, we always put a tree in there, but I haven't decorated it. I thought the children might like to help you do that.'

He felt a lump in his throat. 'Thank you, that's really kind of you. I need to buy some decorations.'

'No, you don't, we've got hundreds,' Andrew said drily. 'Boxes full of them. I'll sort you some out.' He straightened up and stood back, looking at the tree with a critical eye, then nodded. 'Right—teatime?'

'What a good idea. Rory, would you like some apple cake? Freya? Or do you want a boiled egg?'

'Egg and cake,' Rory said, and James opened his mouth to protest, caught Sue's challenging smile and subsided.

Gratefully.

What a day.

Kate arrived back from finishing off her Christmas shopping just as James and the children were straggling back to the barn laden down with boxes.

Well, James was laden. Rory had a bag of what looked like fairy-lights, and Freya was carrying an armful of tinsel.

It was starting to trail, and as she walked towards them, a loop slipped down and Freya caught her foot in it and started to topple.

'Whoops!' she said, scooping up child and tinsel together, and Freya giggled and shoved the tinsel into her face.

'Pretty!' she said, and Kate grinned.

'You are, you're gorgeous.' She kissed her plump rosy cheek. She smelt of apple cake, and Kate realised her mother had been at work again.

'We're going to decorate the tree,' James said a little obviously, and then added, after a slight hesitation, 'Do you want to join us?'

She hesitated, but then Rory tugged at her sleeve. 'You have to, Kate. Please?'

She met James's eyes over the top of the tinsel and searched them for hidden messages, but there didn't seem to be any. He was just asking her if she wanted to join them. Nothing significant. Nothing earth-shattering or meaningful.

'Actually, I've got rather a lot to do,' she said, and then wondered if she'd imagined the withdrawal in his eyes, or if she was just trying to convince herself there was something there when there wasn't.

'I might join you later,' she added, hoping to see a return of that warmth, but it was gone, carefully veiled now, and he nodded.

'Do that—if you've got time. Come on, Rory. We've got a lot to do. Help Freya with the tinsel.'

So she put the toddler down, and she ran after her father and brother, and left Kate standing there alone.

Oh, well. It was her own fault. She could have said yes.

Kicking herself, she unloaded the car and tried not to look into the barn at James and the children unpacking all the decorations and exclaiming in delight.

She could have said yes.

So why hadn't she?

CHAPTER TEN

HE OUGHT to leave her alone.

He'd invited her in, and she'd declined. He couldn't bully her. It was up to her, and she'd said she was busy.

But the communicating door was calling to him from the corner of his eye, and he could hear her moving around.

Doing all the things she had to do. She was probably wrapping a mountain of presents—something he still had to do, if he ever got round to buying paper—and she wouldn't have time for him and his children. She'd probably got a tree of her own to decorate.

But it just seemed wrong, somehow, without her. As if there was someone missing—and, curiously, the someone wasn't Beth. Beth seemed like someone from another lifetime, and he supposed she was.

He thought about it, but decided he didn't feel guilty. Well, he did, about plenty of things, but not Beth. He just felt lonely, and if Kate was there, somehow it would be more fun for all of them.

He was at the door with his hand raised when there was a knock on it, and he pulled it open and gave her a wry smile. 'I was just coming to get you,' he said, and she smiled back and went up on tiptoe and kissed his cheek.

'I'm sorry. I just had some things I needed to do. How far have you got— Oh! It's looking lovely!'

'Not really. It's a bit sparse and a bit lopsided, and the lights aren't quite even, but, hey. We did it.'

She gave him an encouraging smile and headed towards the tree. 'You just need a few more little things on it. Oh— what's this?'

'I made it at school,' Rory told her. 'It's an angel.'

It was an angel, but it was a pretty scruffy angel, he thought. Kate, though, didn't seem to think any such thing.

She moved it to a more prominent position, rummaged in the box and came up with more red baubles and a fairy, and then after they'd put the baubles on in the gaps she made James stand on a chair and hold Freya up so she could put the fairy on the top.

'There!' she exclaimed, laughing. 'Now it's finished.' And she took Freya from him and swung her round, which gave him time to straighten the fairy before he got down and put the chair away.

And swallowed the lump in his throat.

Christmas was coming with the speed of an express train.

They spent part of Tuesday rounding up all their things and taking them through into her house, and changing the sheets ready for the family's arrival the next day, Christmas Eve.

And because she only had one spare room, that meant James would be sleeping with the children.

Still, she consoled herself, it was only for two or three nights. The family never stayed for long—not long enough, really, but this time she realised she'd be glad to see them go.

'Why are we moving into your house?' Rory asked as

they sat down for a drink and a biscuit when all the shuffling was done.

'Because all my brothers and sisters are coming to stay,' she explained. 'There are lots and lots of them, and some of them are married now and have children, so it's busy.'

'Why do you have so many lots?'

She laughed and ruffled his hair. 'Because my parents love children,' she answered honestly, without going into detail. 'You've met Dan and Rachel and little Sean, haven't you?' He nodded. 'They're just coming on Christmas Day. And there's my brother Michael and his wife, Louise—they won't stay over, either, but Angie and Joel and Patrick will be here with their other halves, and Patrick's got four children, and Angie's got two, and then there's Lucy, and I'm not sure about Barney. He might be coming, but he's a pilot so he may not be in England, even.'

'Good grief,' James said, looking stunned. 'Really that many? Where do they put them all?'

'Oh, that's just some of them. Some of them won't come, some will drop in, others just ring. Those are the main contenders, though. The hard-core family members who never miss it, come hell or high water. It's a lot of fun, but we all fit in somehow. I hate it when I'm on duty, but because I work locally, I can usually spend some time here, if not all of it. It's great.'

'That sounds so alien to me. I'm an only child, and Christmas—well, if you blinked, you missed it.'

'Poor you. That's awful.'

'I never thought of it like that. It was just how it was. Your mother must be exhausted by the time they go,' he said a little faintly.

She laughed. 'Actually, she misses them. She loves it.' She tipped her head on one side. 'So—are you all ready?'

'Ready?'

'You know—done the wrapping and so on. When are you seeing your mother?'

'This evening—so I suppose I ought to sort her things out,' he said, looking preoccupied. 'Um—I don't suppose you've got any wrapping paper?'

'Oh, I might have a little left,' she teased, and took it out of the dresser and handed it to him. 'Sticky tape?'

He just smiled, and she found a reel of tape and added it to the pile. 'Bows? Tags?'

He snorted. 'I think that's enough. A couple of tags, maybe. I'll get some later, when we go over there. It's only for her things. I'll do the rest later on, when the children are in bed.'

'Because it's ours?' Rory asked mischievously, and James tweaked his nose and grinned at him.

'Maybe.'

'We're having presents,' he chanted, and she was so relieved to see it, after the Father Christmas letter incident, that she almost joined in.

Then Rory said, 'Will we put them under your tree, or ours?' and she bit her lip.

'I don't have a tree,' she confessed, and James looked stunned.

'You don't? You must have a tree.'

'I haven't. I never bother. There's one next door, and one in the hall in the house, and one in the drawing room—why would I need a tree here, too?'

'Because it's Christmas!' Rory said, horrified. 'Kate, you must. Where will Father Christmas put your presents? Daddy, get her a tree!'

'I think I will,' he said, his face strangely disturbed. 'I'll go and do it now. Come on, kids. We're going tree shopping.'

Kate laughed and stood up. 'We don't go shopping. We grow them on the farm. We'll go and pick one. My uncle Bill will find us a nice one. Come on, then, if you insist. Let's go.'

They bundled up in coats, tramped up through the farm and found her uncle cutting trees in the field behind the Dutch barn.

'I thought Andrew had come and got a tree for your barn?' he said, so she explained.

'Oh. So the children need their own, do they?'

'No, Kate needs one,' Rory explained earnestly, and Bill nodded.

'Right. Well, I quite agree. Let's find a nice tree for Kate, and then you can go and help her decorate it.'

They came back from his mother's armed with presents and found Kate had put the lights on the tree but not the baubles, so they hung them, and then went and retrieved Rory's angel and hung it on the branch at the front, and put all the presents underneath, and then he chivvied the children through the bath and into bed.

They were so tired they fell asleep immediately, and he could easily have joined them.

'I'm shattered,' he said wearily, finding a smile for Kate when he went back down to the kitchen, and she gave him an answering smile and handed him a glass of wine.

'It's been a tough few days,' she said. 'I think we've earned this.'

'Too right,' he said, following her through to the sitting room and settling on her lovely, comfy sofa. 'Oh, bliss. Wake me up if I start snoring.'

She laughed. 'Certainly will. So how was your mother?'

He cracked an eye open, then sat up straighter. 'Curiously happy,' he admitted. 'I think she enjoyed the weekend, and she said she was looking forward to babysitting on Boxing Day night when she gets back from her sister's. Will we be back to normal by then, by the way, or will it still be crowded?'

'Oh, no, I think the barn will be back to normal. The house might not, but most people will have gone.'

He nodded. 'Good. That'll make it easier having her over.' He stretched out his legs and groaned. 'The tree looks nice, by the way.'

'It does. Thank you. I really wouldn't have bothered if you hadn't chivvied me, and I should have thought of the children. It's just that this side of the barn is usually adults, so we don't mind. There are enough trees about the place.'

He chuckled and reached his hand out, threading his fingers through hers. 'I could get used to this,' he said with a sigh. 'Sitting here with you in the evenings while the children are asleep upstairs. It'll be really odd when the boiler's fixed and we go home.'

She shifted slightly, turning towards him, and he moved his head so he could meet her eyes. 'What are you going to do about the consultancy?' she asked quietly.

He searched her eyes, but they were strangely unreadable. 'I don't know. Apply, I think, when the time comes. I thought I was going to have to do something else about child care, but my mother seems to have turned a corner—I don't know, your mother's given her so much confidence, and we're talking now and she realises how much I appreciate what she's doing—I hadn't really told her, and I think she was just over-whelmed. But if she's all right, and happy to do it long term, then I don't see why we can't manage—especially now her sister seems to be on the mend. And it doesn't matter if the kids get attached to her, because she's their grandmother, and they're supposed to.'

And then he thought about Kate, and how the children were getting attached to her, and to this place, and to her parents, and he felt a shiver of unease run over him. Would they be massively disrupted when they moved back to their own house again?

Would he?

Oh, God. He was letting himself get drawn into this fairy-tale life of hers, but it was just a mirage, and when the mist cleared he'd be alone again. If only he could find a way of convincing her to move back with him, but no one in their right mind would want to take on such a complicated family. Especially not someone orderly like Kate, who had a row of boxes she was systematically ticking.

There was no way they were one of her boxes, and no amount of wishful thinking would change that.

'I'm bushed,' he told her. 'I think I need to go to bed.'

'OK. Sleep well, I'll see you tomorrow,' she said, and leaning over, she touched her lips to his.

It was like a spark to tinder.

'Oh, Kate,' he groaned, and threading his hands through her hair, he plundered her eager, willing mouth, his body aching for hers, longing to find solace within it, the peace that came afterwards as they lay sprawled together in those few precious minutes before he returned to his own bed.

What would it be like to have the right to stay with her, to sleep with her, to wake with her?

No. She wasn't interested. She didn't want long term.

In your dreams.

His heart heavy, he eased away, brushing the lightest of kisses over her lips before getting to his feet and staring down at her. 'I'll see you in the morning. Sleep well,' he murmured, and headed for the stairs and solitude.

Christmas Eve at the hospital was chaos.

They had the usual flurry of minor surgical emergencies—two hernias, an appendix, a blocked gall bladder that they cleared using an endoscope and a stent to keep the duct patent, and otherwise they were discharging patients as fast as they reasonably could.

Including Jon, who was making excellent progress and couldn't get out quickly enough.

He wasn't alone. Everybody wanted to go home for Christmas, including the staff, and Kate was a firm believer in recovering in familiar surroundings and with familiar pathogens, instead of hospital bugs and noise and an unusual and busy routine.

So they discharged, and they did admin, and then the ward clerk handed her a handful of post.

'This is for you and Mr McEwan—cards and things.'

'Thank you,' she murmured, and went through to her office. James was just finishing off a discharge letter, and he looked up as she went in.

'Cards for you,' she said, handing him the envelopes, and he slit them open.

'Oh. This is from Jon. "Thank you for all your excellent care. I underestimated what you do. Please pass the enclosed on to the League of Friends. Many thanks." Wow. Big cheque.'

She stared at it and laughed. 'Well, that's a turn-up for the books. Who's the next one from?'

'Tracy,' he said with a grin. 'She's back with her boy-friend, and she's dyed her hair purple. There's a photo of her.'

He flipped it across the desk so she could see it, and then pulled the other card out of the envelope.

She was still looking at the photo of Tracy and her boy-friend, but there was something about his stillness that brought her eyes up from the photo to his face. 'James?'

'It's from Amanda Symes,' he said, his voice like gravel as he read it out. '"Steve died peacefully at home on Sunday. We were all with him. It was very calm and dignified. Thank you for all your support…"'

His voice cracked, and he dropped the card on the desk and pushed his chair back, then swore, quietly but comprehensively.

'Sorry. I was hoping they'd have Christmas together, but maybe it's better this way.' He stood up. 'Right, I've got things to do. I'll catch up with you later.'

She watched him go, his eyes shuttered, and if the phone hadn't been ringing and the ward staff hadn't been clamouring for her attention, she would have put her head down on her desk and howled.

'Happy Christmas!'

Kate prised open her eyes and found Rory standing by her bed, his eyes sparkling with excitement. 'Happy Christmas, sweetheart,' she said, and reaching out for him, she gave him a big hug. 'Where's your daddy?'

'Right here, with a cup of tea for you. I'm sorry about the noise. Happy Christmas.'

She laughed and levered herself up the bed. 'Happy Christmas yourself,' she said, taking the tea from him and drawing him down with her other hand to kiss his cheek, trying to ignore the fact that he was dressed only in a pair of pyjama bottoms hanging loosely on his lean hips. 'So where's Freya?'

'Asleep. It's only six, and the excitement of meeting all the other children last night seems to have worn her out. Not Rory, though. He's as bright as a button.'

'I've got presents under the tree,' he said, clambering up onto her bed and settling down at her feet. 'Lots of them. Are you going to get up?'

'In a minute, when I've had my tea,' she said with a laugh. 'Goodness, you're in a hurry. It's very early.'

'I know,' he said, looking crestfallen. 'Daddy says we have to be quiet because of all the others sleeping in the other house, but I expect they'll want their presents, too, so if we make lots of noise they'll know they can get up and then they'll be happy, too!'

James was rolling his eyes, and she stifled a chuckle. 'Just give me five minutes, Rory, OK? I need to drink my tea and wake up, and then I'll come down.'

'OK,' he said, sliding off the bed and grabbing James by the hand. 'Come on, Daddy, we can go and squash the presents and see if we can guess.'

'Hang on, I need a jumper on, I'm freezing. Now, shush, don't wake Freya.'

They went out, and she listened to Rory trying so hard to be quiet while he was fizzing inside, and smiled.

Oh, she couldn't stay there, lying in her bed while he was so excited. And Freya was stirring, so she pulled on her slipper socks and her dressing-gown, went through to the bedroom next door and lifted her out of the cot, gave her a cuddle and changed her nappy, then took her downstairs.

'Guess who I found?' she said, and Rory jumped up and ran over and gave her a big, slobbery kiss.

'Happy Christmas!' he said, bubbling over with excitement, and Freya wriggled out of her arms and ran over to James and swarmed up him with a huge smile.

'Ch'is'mas!' she said happily, and gave him one of her special baby kisses, and when he looked up at Kate, she could see the happiness in his eyes, and she couldn't help but be glad for him.

If she'd done nothing else, she'd given them this Christmas, and with a new year about to dawn, maybe he'd be able to move on.

It would be without her, she knew that, especially after seeing him yesterday when he'd opened Amanda's card. Beth was still too big a part of their lives, his heart still too raw, but maybe one day…

And then he patted the sofa beside him and invited her over, and her mother's words came back to her.

Of course, you could solve the problem at a stroke.

How?

By volunteering.

For what? To be his nanny?

No. To be his wife.

Could she be the wife he needed? The mother of his children?

Oh, please, God, yes, she thought. But she didn't think he was going to ask her, and she didn't have the courage to volunteer…

They opened their presents, and Kate's eyes filled when she unwrapped her sweater.

'Oh, James—it's like my favourite one! Oh, it's lovely—and it's real cashmere! Oh, you shouldn't.'

No. He probably shouldn't, but it was so pretty, and he loved her so much.

What?

'Go and try it on,' he said, choked, just to get her out of the room, but she shook her head.

'In a minute,' she said, and came over to him and kissed him. Properly. On the lips, in front of his children. 'Thank you.'

'My pleasure,' he said, trying to smile, but emotions were crashing through him and it was all he could do to breathe.

'Here—there's one for Freya,' she said, pulling a present out from under the tree, and gradually his lungs started to work again and his mind began to function and somehow he managed to get through the rest of the happy mayhem without falling apart.

How could he have been so stupid? She didn't want him. She was just being sweet to them all, but she had a life, a career, a grand master plan that didn't include him and his damaged little family, and he'd better remember that.

But then she handed him a present from her—a book on restoring Edwardian houses, and she'd signed it, 'With all my love, Kate.'

With all her love?

Really?

Or was it just a figure of speech?

Something was wrong.

He seemed—what? Distant? Preoccupied? Unhappy?

Missing Beth again, of course. Oh, stupid, stupid her, to imagine she could compete with a ghost.

'Right, everyone, let's get washed and dressed and go over to the house!' she said with what was surely too much enthusiasm, but the children scrambled to their feet and ran for the stairs, and she followed them up, James in her wake, and at the top he stopped her.

'So what happens now?' he asked.

'We normally go over to the house and meet up for coffee, then we head up the hill to the church for the family carol service. Then we all help with lunch, and after that we lie around eating nuts and chocolates and Turkish delight for as long as we can bear it, and then we have tea. It can be quite full on, so I don't know how much of it you want to be involved in.'

His eyes clouded, and he nodded. 'Well—perhaps we should amuse ourselves till lunch, then,' he said, and she realised it had sounded as if she didn't want them.

She gave a quick shake of her head in denial. 'James—I only meant you might find it all a bit much. I didn't want you feeling obliged to join in if you didn't want to. But you're *really* welcome. We want you here.'

'Do you?' he asked, his voice curiously brittle. 'Do you want me here?'

She couldn't lie, but the truth…

'Yes,' she said, giving him the truth in the end, because there was no other way to go. 'Yes, I do want you here. Very much.'

His mouth softened, and he smiled. 'Then we'll come over now, and we'll tough it out, and eat the nuts, and if the children haven't been sick we'll have tea, and then we'll come back here and I'll try to get them to sleep.'

The sweater was gorgeous on her.

It was a perfect fit, and it was as much as he could do to keep his hands to himself and not stroke it. He behaved, though, all through the noisy greetings and the kisses and the bustle and jostle of getting them organised for church, then in the church he was mercifully at one end of a pew with the children between him and Kate, and then at lunch she was seated opposite him next to her brother Michael, so it was easy.

But then later, when the noise had died down and the children were playing a little more sensibly and the adults were sprawled by the fire, he sat in a chair with Freya asleep on his lap and she came and sat down on the floor at his feet and leant against his legs, and he couldn't resist it any more. His hand found her shoulder and squeezed it, and she slid her hand up and caught his fingers and held them, right there in front of all her family.

And it would be so easy to imagine it could last for ever, that he could be here with them next Christmas and the Christmas after and the one after that…

Freya stirred, and he eased his hand away and looked down at Kate's enquiring, upturned face.

'All right?' she asked, and he nodded.

'I'm going to take her back to the barn and change her nappy,' he murmured.

'Want me to come?'

Did he? Was this the time to tell her that he couldn't do this any more, that he needed to get out of here and stop pretending that they belonged, stop playing Happy Families and get back to normal?

'I'm fine,' he said. 'You stay and enjoy your family. Could you keep an eye on Rory for me? We won't be long.'

'Of course.'

He took Freya over to the barn, changed her nappy and lay down with her, but she wouldn't settle again, so he braced himself and went back to the fray.

He was in the sitting room alone, with just the fairy-lights on, and she hesitated in the doorway.

'James?'

He looked up, but she couldn't read his expression in the dark. 'Hi. Is the party finally over?'

'Oh, they'll go on for hours,' she said with a little laugh, 'but Michael and Louise have gone home, so I thought I'd come and keep you company.'

'You don't have to do that.'

Oh, he was so wrong there. She absolutely had to do that. She'd missed him horribly. 'Would you rather be alone?'

'No. Of course not. I've been waiting up for you.'

She went in and perched on the end of the sofa and tried to read his eyes. 'Are you all right?'

'Yes, I'm fine,' he said quietly. 'It's just all a bit—you know. Happy Families.'

Her heart contracted. 'Oh, James. I'm sorry.'

'No, don't be,' he said, reaching for her hand and drawing her down beside him. 'It's been wonderful. The kids have had a brilliant time, and so have I. It's just—well, it would be too easy to get carried along by it, to imagine we're really part of it, but it isn't real, and we'll be going home soon. I mustn't let myself forget that.'

She wished she could read his eyes.

'The other night you said you could get used to it—sitting here with me with the children asleep upstairs,' she said, her heart pounding.

'I could,' he said softly. 'I so easily could. I have. And I'll miss you, when we go. Miss all of you, but you especially. I know you're not interested in us—I mean, why would you be? We're a strange little family, just about managing to keep our heads above water, with a house that needs so much doing to it that if I start now and work every weekend and evening for the next ten years it might almost be fit to live in.'

'Not if you can afford to pay someone to do it. You've got

the job, you know. I saw the clinical director yesterday. They want you, so your money problems are over.'

Her eyes had grown accustomed to the dark, and she saw his rueful smile. Saw it, and didn't really understand it.

'I've got it?' he murmured. 'They haven't even interviewed me yet.'

'Of course they have. And they've seen a few others. They'll want to talk to you formally, of course, but it's yours if you want it.' She felt a sudden fear that he was going to leave. 'You do want it, don't you?'

His laugh sounded bemused. 'Well, yes, of course I want it. It'll be fantastic—but it isn't really the nuts and bolts I was thinking about. Not the house, or the job. It's us.'

'Us?' she echoed, hardly able to breathe.

'Yes, us—if there is an "us". I'm hoping against hope that there is—that there will be. You see, I've just realised, in the last—what, twelve hours or so?—that I love you. And so when I go home without you…'

Her heart lurched. 'You love me?'

'Oh, yes, Kate,' he sighed. 'I love you. But it's OK if it's a problem to you. I won't make it difficult at work, but I thought you ought to know.'

'Oh, James.' She didn't know whether to laugh or cry, so she did both, a funny strangled little sob that could have been either.

'Kate, don't laugh.'

'I'm not. Not really. Only—it's not a problem to me, James, because I love you, too.'

'You love me?'

He sounded stunned, so she reached out a hand and cradled his jaw tenderly. 'Yes, James. I love you. I've told myself it's too early, you're still grieving for Beth, but I think, given time, we could have something good, something solid and decent and—'

'And the children?' he asked, his hand coming up to grip hers where it lay against his cheek. 'Do you love the children?'

'Oh, James,' she whispered unsteadily, tears filling her eyes. 'How could I not love the children? Of course I love the children.'

'This isn't just because of what Rory said? You know, the Father Christmas thing, about wanting a mummy for Christmas? Because I couldn't stand that, you being with us because you pitied us.'

'I don't pity you!' she said, shocked. 'Why would I pity you? OK, you've had a hell of a time, but you've got Rory and Freya, and you're all so close, you love each other so much, and they're yours. Your own family. That's so precious. I've wanted that so much,' she said wistfully.

His arm slid round her shoulders and he hugged her gently. 'I know. I could tell, from the way you talked about kids, from seeing you with mine. You're a natural mother, and it's a wicked waste that you haven't got your own children. You'd be wonderful with them.'

She gave a little huff of laughter. 'I thought, when I married Jon, that maybe I'd have all that, but he was…just wrong for me. So wrong.'

'And you think I could be right?'

'Absolutely right,' she said, hanging on to his hand as if she'd die without the contact. 'You're warm and generous and loving, you don't make judgements, you care about people— I love you, James. I didn't think I'd ever dare to love again, after Jon, but I can't help loving you, or your family. And you aren't a strange little family. You're just sad.'

His lips brushed hers. 'No. We were sad. We aren't sad now, because we've found you, and you've made such a difference to our lives that the idea of going back to our house and leaving you behind is unbearable.'

'Then don't. Stay here, with me while you do up your house. Or take me with you, and we'll live in a muddle. Or I've got another house we could live in, or we could sell both and live here and buy the other barn off my parents and convert it and live in that. I don't care, just so long as I'm with you.'

Kate, shut up! Let him speak. Let him think. Stop talking about nothing.

He laughed softly, and his lips brushed hers. 'I don't care, either. I love you so much,' he murmured. 'I realised it the other night, and I was gutted, because I didn't think there was any way you'd be interested in me. In us.'

'Oh, James, you idiot,' she chided softly, and he laughed again, a little oddly, and squeezed her hand.

'Yeah. I am, aren't I? A real fool. And sitting here in the dark waiting for you to come home, I seem to have turned into an optimistic fool,' he said, then, easing away from her, he stood up and walked towards the door.

'James?' she said, fear and confusion gripping her as he walked away, but he just put the lights on low so they could see each other and turned round and came back to her, kneeling down in front of her and taking her hand, that slightly crooked, uncertain smile a little unsteady.

'Marry me, Kate—if you really mean it, and you really love me in the way that I love you—that the sun won't shine and the night never ends if I'm not with you—then marry me. I put the past behind me ages ago. I loved Beth, and there'll always be a special place for her in my heart, but in a way I let her go when she was diagnosed. And then I was so busy with the practical stuff that before I knew it, it didn't really hurt any more. It's the present that's been getting me down, but since I've met you everything's changed. It feels as if the sun's come out again, and all I can think about is the future—with you.'

He pressed her fingers to his lips. 'I love you. I need you. We need you. Be part of our family. Extend it—or not. Whatever you want, because I can't live without you, Kate. I need you, more than I need air. You're my heart, my soul. My life. My love.'

'Oh, James.'

His eyes were bright, the pale blue shimmering with emotion, and she leant forwards and touched her lips to his.

'Is that a yes? Please, tell me it's a yes.'

'Yes, my love,' she said. 'Yes, it's a yes. I'll marry you, because I need you, too—all three of you. And I can't live without you, either. But I have to warn you, I do want children of my own. And maybe other people's, too. I'm afraid I'm a bit like my mother.'

He smiled. 'A full house, every Christmas, till the end of our days?'

She laughed a little unevenly. 'Probably, so your lovely house may not be big enough for us for very long. Can you bear it?'

He drew her into his arms and hugged her tight. 'It sounds wonderful,' he said softly, and then lifting his head, he stared down into her eyes and smiled.

'Happy Christmas, my love,' he murmured, and kissed her…

MILLS & BOON

MEDICAL

On sale 2nd January 2009

THE SINGLE DAD'S NEW-YEAR BRIDE
by Amy Andrews

It began with a magical midnight kiss at a New Year Ball...
and that's where paediatric nurse Hailey Winters knows it
should end. But it's too late – she's already fallen for the sexy
Head of Paediatrics, Callum Craig – and his adorable child...

THE WIFE HE'S BEEN WAITING FOR
by Dianne Drake

Michael Sloan's brilliant career as a surgeon ended after he was
badly injured. Now, a ship's doctor, he has avoided emotional
entanglements – until beautiful passenger Dr Sarah Collins
makes Michael believe that he is, most definitely,
a man worth loving.

POSH DOC CLAIMS HIS BRIDE
by Anne Fraser

When Meagan arrives as the new GP on Scotland's Western
Isles, she doesn't expect to meet Dr Cameron Stuart.
Cameron is the man who broke her heart six years earlier –
and she's just discovered he's a lord as well as a single father!
For Cameron this is his chance to follow his heart and
claim Meagan as his new Lady Grimsay!

Newborn babies will bring three couples together

...in the most surprising circumstances!

Stranded with a gorgeous stranger...
Rescued by a rich man...
Snowed in with her billionaire boss...

Available 2nd January 2009

www.millsandboon.co.uk

Celebrate 100 years of pure reading pleasure with Mills & Boon®

To mark our centenary, each month we're publishing a special 100th Birthday Edition. These celebratory editions are packed with extra features and include a FREE bonus story.

Plus, you have the chance to enter a fabulous monthly prize draw. See 100th Birthday Edition books for details.

Now that's worth celebrating!

September 2008

Crazy about her Spanish Boss by Rebecca Winters
Includes FREE bonus story
Rafael's Convenient Proposal

November 2008

The Rancher's Christmas Baby
by Cathy Gillen Thacker
Includes FREE bonus story *Baby's First Christmas*

December 2008

One Magical Christmas by Carol Marinelli
Includes FREE bonus story *Emergency at Bayside*

Look for Mills & Boon® 100th Birthday Editions at your favourite bookseller or visit
www.millsandboon.co.uk

FREE!

4 Books
and a surprise gift!

We would like to take this opportunity to thank you for reading this Mills & Boon® book by offering you the chance to take FOUR more specially selected titles from the Medical™ series absolutely FREE! We're also making this offer to introduce you to the benefits of the Mills & Boon® Book Club™—

- ★ **FREE home delivery**
- ★ **FREE gifts and competitions**
- ★ **FREE monthly Newsletter**
- ★ **Exclusive Mills & Boon Book Club offers**
- ★ **Books available before they're in the shops**

Accepting these FREE books and gift places you under no obligation to buy, you may cancel at any time, even after receiving your free shipment. Simply complete your details below and return the entire page to the address below. You don't even need a stamp!

YES! Please send me 4 free Medical books and a surprise gift. I understand that unless you hear from me, I will receive 6 superb new titles every month for just £2.99 each, postage and packing free. I am under no obligation to purchase any books and may cancel my subscription at any time. The free books and gift will be mine to keep in any case.

M8ZEF

Ms/Mrs/Miss/Mr ....Initials ....

Surname ....
BLOCK CAPITALS PLEASE

Address...

....

....Postcode.............................

Send this whole page to:
UK: FREEPOST CN8I, Croydon, CR9 3WZ